OPERATION OVERLORD

OPERATION OVERLORD

A TOMMY COLLINS ADVENTURE

a novel

francis moss

ACKNOWLEDGEMENTS

Thanks especially to my wife Phyllis, whose patience with me ("Not now, I'm writing!") and critical eye helped make my writing as good as I can make it. Thanks to my early readers and critics: our daughter Caitlin, Bea Chambers, Mike Vail, and Martin Milas. Your comments and suggestions were extremely helpful.

Thanks to Laura Garwood & Kristen Hall-Geisler of Indigo Editing, whose sympathetic and thoughtful responses guided me in shaping my storytelling and character-making.

Thanks to Jose Ramirez at Pedernales Publishing, who held my sweaty hand on the path to this and my other books, and who gently steered me in the right direction when I wanted to go left (I'm left-handed; it's a habit).

Thanks to Brian Schwartz of Self-Publish.org, who told me that everything I thought I knew about marketing my books was just the beginning.

Thanks to the members of the Desert Writers Guild, all of whom were helpful in more ways than I can count.

To friends and fellow writers whom I've left out, and who will be sure to tell me that I forgot to mention them. Apologies.

CONTENTS

CHAPTER 1

Thursday, 1 June 1944

It was football day, called Winkies, at Winchester College, the last game of the year. The twelve-year-old boys from Beloe's house, all in their bright red shirts, ran like a gaggle of mad geese out of Winchester College's ancient stone gate and onto Chapel Road. Mr. Simpson, the school's porter and watchman (whom some boys joked had been here since the fourteenth century, when Winchester was founded), stood aside to let them pass, calling out, "Careful, lads. The cobbles are slippery."

Above the ancient brick-and-stone buildings of the college, clouds from the night's rain began to scatter, clearing the day for the game.

As they crossed the street, Tommy Collins ran faster to catch up to red-haired George "Stumpy" Ward, Tommy's best friend at the school, and a fair player.

"This is our last chance to show those Collegemen what our house is capable of," Tommy said.

Stumpy nodded. "We can beat them."

The boys stopped while Housemaster Lymes, in grass-stained pants and striped shirt instead of his usual black robes, unlatched the wooden gate set in the moss-covered stone wall bordering the walkway. Lymes waved his arm. "Hurry, lads," he said. "This weather might change at any moment."

The boys ran through the gate and onto the pitch, a wide green field still soggy from the rain. It was bordered with oak and elm trees as old as the school itself.

The boys from Toye's House were already there, wearing blue jerseys. They stood to one side of the canvas near the netting that kept the ball on the grounds, preventing it from going into Palmer Swamp.

The teams formed up, one at each end of the pitch. Lymes blew his whistle, and the game began. Stumpy forwarded the ball to Tommy. He kicked it downfield toward the opposing goal, called "Worms." Felton, a lad from College, snatched it up and ran down the field to the goal.

Tommy called out the foul: "Handiwork! Handiwork!" He stepped in front of Felton to block his progress. "Taking more than three steps whilst holding the ball is against the rules."

Tommy looked to Housemaster Lymes for support, but the man's attention was elsewhere. Every boy on both sides stared up into the thinning clouds, recognizing the sound of an aircraft engine. Reynolds, the house kicker, shouted, "Doodlebug!" and started running across the field toward the gate. The town air raid sirens began to wail.

The engine noise grew louder. Then the craft descended below the clouds: not the doodlebug (a nickname for the German V-1 aerial bomb) Reynolds thought it was, but a German fighter plane. It was speckled with green, brown, and olive camouflage paint, the swastika clearly visible on the wings and tail. It was coming in low, not two hundred yards away, and heading for the muddy field. Its engine had stopped, and the propeller fluttered. Its fuselage was peppered with bullet holes.

"Form up quickly!" the housemaster called. "Back to the College!"

Most of the boys obeyed, but a half-dozen of them, Beloe's and Toye's houses alike, stood and stared at the descending plane. It looked like it was going to plough into the field near Saint Catherine's Hill.

The boys ran towards the hill. "A Focke-Wulf," Tommy said as he ran up beside Stumpy. Tommy was almost always sure he was right, even when he was wrong. By now, almost every boy could identify the Nazi planes that threatened their country.

But Stumpy corrected him. "It's a Messerschmitt. An ME-109. Look at the pilot's canopy."

As he spoke, the enemy plane, which was in fact a Messerschmitt, landed hard on the grass. Its landing gear collapsed as it slid sideways and its wing hit a tree. The plane crashed into another tree near the foot of the hill. Its tail tilted upward from the sudden stop. The town's sirens wound down like tired banshees. A moment later, they blew the long blast that proclaimed all clear.

A few boys dashed over to the deep furrows dug into the greensward by the plane. They looked for bits of landing gear, pieces of the broken wing—anything that might make a good souvenir. There was a brisk underground trade in such things at the school, and the Housemasters turned a blind eye to most of it. But possession of dangerous items was grounds for discipline or suspension.

There was a reason for this. Two years before, when German aerial attacks were frequent, a fifth form boy exploring the War Cloister had found a live machine gun cartridge that apparently had fallen from a plane, and he and his friends decided to detonate it. During quiet time, they broke into the Works building and clamped the round in a vise. Holding a nail to the primer, they hit it with a hammer. The round had gone through the glass of the Works door, across the grounds, and into the Porter's Lodge, which fortunately was unoccupied at the time.

Just as the boys approached the downed plane, an olive-green military lorry, its rear bed covered by canvas, sped onto the field and slid to a stop between the students and the plane. Its tires dug ruts in the damp sod. A half-dozen Home Guard men leaped out—or slowly climbed down, depending on their age—from the rear and lined up around the plane, keeping the boys at bay. A minute later, an ambulance with a red cross in a white circle on its side arrived. The driver and a Royal Army Medical Corpsman got out and hurried to the plane.

Tommy ran as close as he could to the plane. He was able to see the German pilot slumped in the cockpit. He appeared to be wounded, perhaps dead. Before Tommy could see anything more, a bearded Home Guardsman waved him back. "Move along, lad. Back to school with you."

Tommy backed away reluctantly. Other boys were coming across the field to see the plane, but they too were quickly stopped by the Guardsmen, who had set up a perimeter around the downed aircraft.

Stumpy and Tommy walked across the field towards the footbridge. Most of the others had gone ahead.

"A bit of excitement today," Stumpy said with a crooked grin.

"Yes, but now we won't be able to finish our game," Tommy replied. "Leave-out is next week, and we have exams." Pointing to the deep furrows in the grass, he added, "And look at our pitch. It's all a mess."

As Stumpy and Tommy walked back to the gate, they heard a boy shout, "Let me go! Let me go!"

Tommy turned off the path and headed to the grove of trees along the Itchen Stream. Stumpy followed. Cyril Hightower stood with two of his fellow bullies on the other side of the stream amidst three ten-year-old lads. There were twigs floating down the stream. The younger boys had been at Poohsticks, a game played by dropping small willow branches from the upstream side of a bridge then running to the bridge's downstream side. The winner was the boy whose stick first appeared.

Hightower stood on the stream bank holding Elton, one of the boys, by his waist and suspending him over the water. "I'll let you go right now. Perhaps you'll be a Poohstick yourself, Elton," he laughed. The two bullies pushed the remaining younger lads away, daring them to do something.

"Say, Hightower, why don't you pick on someone your own size?" Tommy said.

"Where's the fun in that?" he replied with a short laugh. He shook Elton as he dangled over the water. The younger boy started sniffling. Hightower mocked him: "Oh, you're not going all lobster on us, are you?"

Tommy strode over to confront him. Stumpy followed reluctantly. "Put Elton down, Hightower," Tommy said.

"Or what, Collins?" Hightower replied. "You are somewhat outnumbered, you know. Besides, Elton's my servant. I can do as I choose with him." Hightower shook Elton again, harder. "Isn't that right, boy?" Elton's only reply was a sniffle.

The bullies turned away from the younger lads. They surrounded Tommy and menaced Stumpy, who turned and walked to the gate, looking over his shoulder. After a moment of glaring and threats, Tommy pushed Hightower towards the water with one hand. As Hightower struggled to regain his balance, Tommy seized Elton with the other. Hightower loosened his grip, and Tommy pulled the smaller boy to the streambank.

Hightower stumbled backwards and fell with a splash into the stream. The water was only a few inches deep, and Hightower stood up at once, enraged, his school pants soaking wet. "Get Collins! Thrash him!" he ordered his minions.

Just then, one of Hightower's friends looked down the path. "The housemaster's coming!"

The younger boys took the opportunity to escape. A moment later, Housemaster Lymes crossed the wooden bridge. He stopped and looked at Tommy, Hightower, and the bullies.

"What's this about, now?"

"Just leaving, sir," Hightower said. He turned to Tommy and snarled in a low voice, "You'll suffer for this, Collins! I promise it." He and his friends turned and walked away.

Tommy looked for Stumpy, but he had vanished. He continued back toward the school. As he crossed Kingsgate Street, Stumpy came out of L. B. James's Sweet Shop and held out a paper cone with lollies in it.

"Have some," he said, sucking on a sweet.

Tommy took a lemon drop. "You might have stood by me back there, Stumpy" he said, knowing that it would do little good.

"I...I am sorry, Tom," he replied. "Cyril and his gang are vicious. I heard they beat one of the second formers so badly he was put in hospital."

"I heard that too," Tommy said, "but I think I could hold my own in a set-to with Hightower." Tommy was to find that out—sooner than he expected.

CHAPTER 2

By the time Tommy and Stumpy got back to school, the clouds had returned, bringing a spring drizzle with them. They dashed across the wet cobblestones of Kingsgate Road, ran under the ancient stone archway, sprinted across the grassy commons, and burst into Toye's House. The nineteenth-century brick structure was hot in the summer and cold in the winter. Drafts blew through cracks in the window frames and along corridors and managed to find their way into every room, creeping under the too-thin covers of every shivering boy.

Tommy and Stumpy shared a room with ten other second form boys. Their beds were metal cots with bedding supplied by the school. They had extra blankets provided by parents and Old Wykehamists—former Winchester students, many of whom were now at war.

"Supper in half an hour," Tommy said. He pulled his jacket and shirt off the narrow rack that served as a closet for the junior boys in the dormitory. He tossed his damp and grass-stained football shorts on his bed.

"I know. And I'm famished," Stumpy replied as he buttoned up his shirt and put on his tie.

The boys hurried downstairs as the bell rang, signaling mealtime. The grubbing hall was, as usual, crowded and noisy. A dozen boys lined up for servings of thin cabbage and potato soup, a slice of bread, and "steamed to death" carrots. The war rationing meant that all the boys were hungry, all the time. Housemaster pointed out that the number of "corpulent," as he called them, students had decreased somewhat, although visits to the sweet shop had not declined. Even sugar was rationed. Donations of fruits and biscuits from parents and alumni were rare and welcome. They had become a kind of currency in exchange for favors: "Do translate this Cicero poem for me, and I'll give you a Fry's chocolate."

The talk at dinner was all about the downed German plane. A half-dozen unrecognizable parts were passed around the tables. "This was part of the wing!"

"Don't be silly. It's from the aileron."

After midday meal, Tommy and Stumpy had history. The classroom, just off the quad, was a high-ceilinged, grey-walled room with windows that rattled and shook when the wind blew.

"Today we begin our study of the Magna Carta," Mr. Symmes, the Latin and Greek instructor, began. He shoved his rimless glasses up the bridge of his nose for the fifth time since class had begun. "Who knows what that means?" he asked.

Tommy raised his hand.

"Master Collins?"

"It means 'big wagon,'" Tommy said with more assurance than he felt. A few boys chuckled.

Mr. Symmes smiled. "Your former school didn't teach you Latin?"

"No sir," Tommy replied. He wasn't exactly lying. His school in London had Latin classes that Tommy attended—whilst successfully managing to avoid learning anything.

"Well, you get half-credit. Magna Carta means 'the Great Charter.' 'Big wagon' would be 'magna plaustra,' or 'magnum carrum.'"

He wrote *Magna Carta Libertatum* on the blackboard. "The Magna Carta, the great charter of liberties," Mr. Symmes continued, "is perhaps one of the most important gifts England has given the world. It has been called the bible of the English Constitution."

The lesson went on. Tommy and the other nine boys in class dutifully wrote in their notebooks. Mr. Symmes pushed his glasses up on his nose.

After history, the boys had mugging time, a free hour to spend on their studies. But Tommy usually devoted the hour to exploring the campus and avoiding the prefects patrolling the quad in their robes with their watchful eyes.

In the quad, Rogers, a second form boy, hailed Tommy. "I heard about your set-to with Hightower," Rogers said. "Good on you. But he's a vengeful sort. You would be wise to watch your back."

"Thanks, Rogers. I'll be on my guard," Tommy said.

Tommy decided to take his stroll before it got too dark. Wartime blackouts made night-time explorations an adventure, especially with the puddles on the green. Tommy crossed the quad, hurrying back to Toye's House, as the sun was setting behind the chapel.

"There you are, Collins!" Hightower stepped out from the shadows under the stone entry arch.

Tommy, acting braver than he felt, stood his ground. "Well, at least you have the courage to show up without your usual companions."

"I don't need them," Hightower said, curling his lip. "I can deal with a rude child all by myself." He charged suddenly at Tommy, pushing him against the rough-hewn granite wall and putting his arm against his chest to hold him.

Tommy struggled, but Hightower was bigger and stronger. Hightower raised his fist, but Tommy grabbed the arm holding him and pushed as hard as he could while ducking his head to one side.

Hightower swung, and his fist smashed into the granite, narrowly missing Tommy's face. He stepped back, bent over, and clutched his hand, which was bruised and bloody. "Damn you! Damn you!" Hightower said. He turned his head and called, "Jones!"

Suddenly Tommy was gripped from behind, with strong hands holding his arms. He struggled and turned his head to see Welshy Jones, a pimply faced boy and Hightower's companion. "Got you, you little bastard!"

"Hold him tight! He's a slippery one," Hightower said, stepping forward so he was inches away from Tommy.

"Couldn't do it by yourself after all, you coward," Tommy said. He got a punch in the ear from Jones as an answer. Tommy tried to break free, but the best he could do was to stomp on Jones's foot, which earned him a twist of his arms behind his back. They felt like they might break. Hightower yanked Tommy free of Jones's grasp and threw him down into a puddle.

Suddenly a bright light lit up the three. "What's this?" a voice said. Tommy recognized it as Prefect Conover, in charge of the boys at college.

Hightower held up his hand, shielding his eyes against the light. "Please sir, shine that torch away."

Conover, in robe and slippers, hurried across the grass, the torch bobbing as he approached.

Hightower nudged Jones, who stepped forward. "I was heading to my house when I saw Collins here attacking Hightower."

Tommy got to his feet, dripping with muddy water. "That's a lie!" he said. "The two of them overpowered me."

Conover waved his flashlight. "Come along. We'll sort this out with the headmaster."

Headmaster Leeson's oak-paneled office seemed to Tommy to be designed to intimidate visitors. The walls were covered with ancient-looking, gilt-framed portraits of past headmasters and ancient-looking, black-framed parchment declarations in Latin. In a place of honor was a portrait of William of Wykeham, the school's founder. A wooden plaque hung on the wall behind the Headmaster's desk, with the school's motto inscribed: *Manners maketh man.*

The last time Tommy had been here, when he was admitted to Winchester last fall, he was awed. Now he felt torn between fear and the rightness of his cause.

Leeson came into the room, tying the belt of his dressing gown. "What's all this?" he asked in his gruff voice, looking hard at Conover and the three disheveled boys.

Conover cleared his throat. "A bit of a dustup, sir."

"Looks more like a mud-up," Leeson said as he nodded at Tommy, a hint of a smile on his face.

Hightower stepped forward, holding up his bloody hand. "Look, sir! Collins attacked me! For no reason!"

"You're a liar and a bully, Hightower!" Tommy cried out.

Leeson pulled out his desk chair and sat down. "All you boys should be in your rooms now." He cleared his throat. "I heard from Housemaster Lymes about an incident after Winkies this morning," he said. "It seems, Mr. Collins, that you have had more than one run-in with Hightower."

"He pushed me into the Itchen!" Hightower said, looking injured.

"Not quite the way I heard it," Leeson said. "Needless to say, we shall pursue this further. Tomorrow morning. At ten o'clock. Your parents' attendance will be required."

"My father's a very busy man…" Hightower began, with a superior smile.

"We are all very busy. It's wartime," Leeson interrupted. "Your continued attendance at Winchester will be discussed."

CHAPTER 3

Conover escorted Tommy back to his dormitory, where Stumpy was anxiously waiting for him with questions. "What happened? Are you sent down?"

Tommy was too tired to answer. "I'll find out in the morning," was all he could say.

He showered in cold water—all there was at that hour—to get the mud out of his hair. He tried his best to wash the dirt off his jacket and pants and hung them up to dry. Despite his feeling that he was in the right, he knew that right did not always triumph. Hightower would have his toady Welshy to back up his story.

Tommy was awake before dawn. He wasn't sure if the prospect of facing the headmaster or facing his parents was the more daunting. He put on his still-damp jacket and pants, brushed his teeth, and was the first in line at breakfast: tea, oatmeal and canned peaches.

Lieutenant Commander Lawrence Collins was already waiting outside the headmaster's office. As

Tommy came up the stairs, he saw his father sitting straight as a ramrod in his Royal Navy dress blue uniform with the two wide and one narrow gold stripes on the jacket cuffs. His black cap, with its badge and shiny brim, was perched on his knee, and his thick-soled black boots had been polished so they gleamed. His father turned as Tommy approached. He didn't smile. Tommy wanted to run down the stairs and outside, away from what was coming. But he came forward.

"Hullo, Dad."

His father patted the empty chair next to him. Tommy sat, awaiting the executioner's axe.

"Tell me what happened," his father said. Tommy took a deep breath, then told the whole story, from the downed German plane, the incident with Hightower at the Itchen, and Hightower's ambush the previous night.

His father nodded. "It's a bit of what I expected," he said. "I don't know this Hightower lad, but I know his father." He turned away, muttering something under his breath that sounded like "two peas in a pod."

Tommy wiggled in his chair, glancing over at the closed door.

Just then Leeson's office door opened, and Mrs. Trimble, the school matron, came out, wearing her usual flowered dress and too much perfume. "He's ready for you, sir. Master Collins may wait here."

Commander Collins got up, straightened his blue jacket, tucked his cap under his arm, and disappeared through the doorway.

"I want to be out of here in ten minutes, do you understand?" Heavy footsteps echoed up the stairs, and two men came into view. One, thin and harried-looking, was nodding. Tommy immediately knew the other one: the elder Hightower, a portly, fleshy-faced, balding man with a pencil moustache. Tommy couldn't resist a smile. Now he knew what Cyril was going to look like in a few years.

Hightower senior half-turned his head. "Hurry up, will you?" Cyril appeared then, hastening to catch up to his father.

Neither Hightower so much as glanced Tommy's way as they passed him. The elder Hightower's harried aide peeked over at him, then almost got hit by the office door as it swung closed in his face. He pushed it open and went in.

Tommy couldn't sit any more. He got up and paced the hall, his shoes echoing on the wooden floor. Minutes dragged on. Tommy hoped he'd have the chance to tell his side of the story.

Another minute and Hightower junior and senior came out, walking quickly, again ignoring Tommy. "Outrageous! Doesn't he know how much I contribute to this school?"

The harried young man followed. "I'm sure he must—"

Hightower senior interrupted, turning to Cyril. "And you sat there like a stone, saying nothing in your defense," he said to his son.

Cyril stammered, "You… You were doing so well, Father. I didn't want to interrupt."

"Pshaw!" Hightower senior said as the three of them went down the stairs.

Mrs. Trimble stuck her head out the office door. "Your turn, Master Collins."

Tommy went in, wiping his sweaty hands on his pants. Headmaster Leeson was seated behind his desk, wearing his funny eyeglasses. They had no earpieces but were held on by gripping either side of his nose, leaving permanent red marks. "Pince-nez," Tommy's mother had called the spectacles, sounding like "pants-nay."

Tommy took a deep breath. His father was seated in a wooden chair across from Leeson. Trimble was on a chair in the corner, writing on a notepad.

Leeson adjusted his spectacles. "I've heard Master Hightower's story of the incident. Now it's your turn, Master Collins."

Tommy took another deep breath, then recited the events, beginning with his rescue of the first form boy and ending with Cyril's attack in the quad.

When Tommy had finished, Leeson adjusted his spectacles and looked up at Tommy and his father. "We have two contradictory narratives here," he said. "Master Collins, you are the villain of Hightower's, and he is the villain of yours. Young Elton has gone home, but I will speak to him.

"We take a serious view of bullying here at Winchester, but we know it goes on. Nevertheless, Collins, you stepped over the line yesterday. The housemaster was nearby. You should have called on him rather than taking matters into your own hands. As for the events of last evening…Well, despite Hightower's claim, and Master Jones's confirmation, that you attacked first, I've decided to let that go."

"But—" Tommy began.

Leeson held up his hand. "I am suspending both you and Hightower. End of term is next week, and you'll be able to make up your work in the fall."

Tommy's father stood up. "That seems fair, Headmaster. Especially considering Mr. Hightower's generous contributions to Winchester."

Leeson's face turned red. "Mr. Hightower played no role in my decision!" He bent down and began going through the papers on his desk, waving his hand in dismissal.

Tommy followed his father out the door. Mrs. Trimble stared at them. The headmaster grumbled something.

They walked across the quad and through the stone arch to St. Cross Road, where the family car, an elderly dark-blue Humber Snipe saloon, was parked.

"That was a good one, Dad," Tommy said, looking up at his father.

Lieutenant Commander Collins just pointed to the dormitory. "Get your things."

Tommy, chastened, ran to the ancient stone building. He returned a few minutes later, loaded down with his clothes and toiletries.

It was a silent drive home. Tommy was convinced he'd done the right thing, but perhaps his father didn't think so.

"Dad…" Tommy began.

"Your mother will be upset," his father interrupted. "She worked very hard to get you into Winchester when we moved here."

"Cyril and his gang are bullies!" Tommy exclaimed. "I was in the right!"

"Sometimes being in the right doesn't matter," his father said. "You still have to do the right thing."

Lawrence pulled into the graveled drive of their rented house on St. Cross Road. "I have an errand," he told Tommy. "I'll be back for supper."

Tommy got out of the Humber and ran to the house. A scudding wind blew clouds overhead.

CHAPTER 4

Friday, 2 June 1944

The Collins family had been living in London when Tommy's father was posted by the admiralty to Portsmouth, on the southeast coast of the English Channel. There had been rumors of an imminent Allied invasion of Europe since early in the year, but no one knew when it would take place or where the landing would be. But with his father making frequent trips to Portsmouth and Southampton, the two major embarkation ports on England's southeast coast, Tommy guessed that the departure point was most certainly there, a bit over one hundred miles from the French coast.

It had been a relief to Margaret, Tommy's mum, when Lawrence got his post. Moving out of London meant the family would be safe from German bombs, which had killed thousands of people. British and Allied air superiority had all but eliminated the Luftwaffe, the

German air force. As a result, the daily bombing raids had stopped, but many people were still worried about aerial attacks.

Tommy watched his father drive off in the Humber, then went into the kitchen to make himself some bread and jam. No one was home. His mum was away doing some defense work; his sister, Olivia, was at school. He was relieved not to face his mum just yet.

As he took the last bite of bread and jam, he heard a crash coming from his father's office. Tommy ran in. A breeze from the window had blown his father's papers off his scratched wooden desk and onto the floor. Tommy shut the window and latched it, then knelt on the floor and began collecting the papers. He knew better than to read top-secret documents, but he couldn't resist a peek. A pinned-together sheaf of papers was labeled "Mulberry Harbours." A folder had been stamped in red, "Most Secret," which Tommy dared not open.

Tommy rose and put the papers back on his father's desk. He looked over at the bookshelf. A thin, grey book with the title *All-in Fighting*, lay on its side on the shelf.

Tommy sat on the floor with the book in his lap. A drawing of two men grappling with one another was on the cover. He opened the book.

Some readers may be appalled at the suggestion that it should be necessary for human beings of the twentieth century to revert to the grim brutality of the stone age in order to live. But it must be realized that, when dealing with an utterly ruthless enemy who has clearly expressed his intention of wiping this nation out of existence, there is no room for any scruple or compunction about the methods to be employed in preventing him.

Tommy heard his father's Humber coming up the lane. He got up from the floor and ran to the living room, where he tucked the book under a sofa cushion. He hurried outside just as his dad turned into the drive. He ran over and hopped up onto the running board as the car pulled into the covered portico.

"Very dangerous, Tommy," his father said as he came to a stop in the drive next to the kitchen.

"I'm careful, Dad," Tommy said, jumping down as his father opened the car door. "I've been practicing on the porch."

His father tried not to smile as he took his pale-grey leather briefcase from the passenger seat, an item, Tommy had noted, that was never out of his sight since they had come to Winchester in March.

"I spoke to your mother," his father said. "We'll discuss your future at supper."

Tommy winced. It sounded ominous. As his father headed to the door, Tommy grabbed his sleeve. "The window in your office blew open. I picked up the papers that were on the floor. I didn't read anything."

Lawrence nodded, smiling. "Good. I wouldn't want to report you to Naval Intelligence." He went into his office with his briefcase and closed the door.

Tommy took *All-in Fighting* from under the sofa cushion and went up to his room to await sentencing.

A few hours later, Tommy heard the rattle of his mother's bicycle. He looked out his bedroom window to see her lean it against the wall of the house and enter the side door with a cloth bag full of whatever groceries she could find at the market.

Rationing had made things difficult during the war. Tommy had fond memories of beef stews and, at Christmas, a wonderful goose with bread pudding for dessert. Now they were lucky to have meat more than once or twice a week, and despite his sister's urgings to buy "privately" from some of the local farmers who sidestepped the strict rationing laws, his mother always said, "Why should we have when others are doing without?"

Despite her family's rules, Olivia did come home at Easter with a dozen eggs she swore she'd found on the road. She soon confessed that by "the road" she meant the nearby farm, where she'd convinced a small girl to trade them for her battered copy of Jane Austen's *Emma*. As a result, Olivia had spent the next three days in her room, and her friends were turned away at the door.

Lieutenant Commander Collins came into the kitchen, which smelled of boiling potatoes, took off his cap and kissed his wife on the cheek. "How was your day, my dear?" He asked.

Mum put down her spoon and wiped her hand across her forehead, tucking a stray lock of reddish-blond hair behind her ear. She was tall, almost as tall as her husband, with a wide smile and an easy laugh—except for now. "Well, at the lodge we wrapped bandages in the morning, then I went to the hospital, which has been overwhelmed by the wounded. A lot of poor young men, some gravely injured," she said shaking her head.

"And more to come, I'm afraid," Lawrence said.

Tommy came into the kitchen. "Is it the invasion, Dad?" Dad put his finger to his lips, and Tommy regretted his outburst. "It's all Most Secret, I know. Sorry," he said.

"You don't talk of my work at the school, do you?" Lawrence looked intently at his son.

"Never! I swear!"

"All right, then," his father replied.

"Supper in half," Mum said. She turned to look at Tommy. "And afterwards we'll have a conversation about your behavior, Thomas." She sighed and turned back to the pot on the stove.

Tommy hung his head. Mum only called him Thomas when she was unhappy with him. He took her sigh as an invitation for him to be ashamed. He wasn't but thought the wiser course of action would be silence.

"It's not much, Maggie," Lawrence said. "Leave-out is next week, and Leeson said Tommy would be able to make up exams come fall term."

Margaret sighed again. "But fighting…"

"I didn't start the fight!" Tommy exclaimed. "Hightower was bullying a first-termer!"

"The world is filled with bullies," his mum said. "You can't fight them all."

"You could have gone to the headmaster," his dad added.

"Hightower lied about what happened in the quad. Headmaster wouldn't believe me," Tommy replied. "I guess he had to punish us both."

"As your mother said, bullies are everywhere," Lawrence said. As Tommy opened his mouth to speak, his father held up his hand. "We're fighting the worst bullies in the world right now."

"The Nazis!" Tommy exclaimed.

"And everything else has to be put to the side." Lawrence turned to his wife. "I think our son had a good reason to do what he did. Perhaps being sent down is enough punishment."

Margaret nodded. "I suppose. Supper's ready. Go wash up, Tommy, then come help set the table."

Tommy, glad to be excused, ran up the narrow wooden stairs with the wobbly banister to the loo, where he splashed water on his face and wiped his hands on a towel, leaving a smear of dirt on it.

Tommy was setting the table when Olivia, sixteen, with her blond hair tied in two braids, came in. "Hullo, all," she said as she dropped her schoolbooks on the green padded chair in the entry hall.

"Take them upstairs, please," Margaret said. "And wash up."

With a grumble, Olivia grabbed her books and ran up the stairs. She came back down a minute later. "What's for supper?"

"Same as yesterday. Same as the day before," Tommy replied. "Potatoes and vegetables with something similar to meat."

Lawrence, sitting in the living room reading the *Times,* chuckled. "There's nothing wrong with Spam," he said.

"As long as you don't read the label," Margaret added, making Lawrence chuckle again.

The family sat down at the dinner table. Mum held out her arms, and they clasped hands and bowed their heads. "Please protect this family," Margaret said.

"And beat the Nazis," Tommy added.

"And help me pass my history next week," Olivia added.

As supper was ending, Olivia looked over at her brother. "I hear you got an arse-whipping at college," she said with a grin.

"Olivia! Language!" Lawrence said, looking at her with a frown.

"I'm just repeating what Hazel told me. Her brother's a collegeman."

"I gave as good as I got," Tommy said. "And there were three of them," he said, adding one other assailant. After all, Hightower had probably had another minion lying in wait.

Lawrence turned to Margaret. "How's Woman's Home Defense going, dear?"

Woman's Home Defense, or WHD, was a nonofficial organization of women across Great Britain who patrolled their neighborhoods, used opera glasses to watch the skies for German planes, and—in a few cases—trained themselves to shoot with their husbands' or fathers' ancient hunting rifles. The most well-known women's group was the Amazon Defense Corps in London, whose members included Marjorie

Foster, the first woman to win the King's Prize for her shooting skills.

Margaret shrugged, tilting her head to one side. "All right, I suppose." From her expression, Tommy knew that it wasn't actually all right.

"Have you spoken to the defense corps head yet?"

Mum pressed her lips tightly together. "That's another thing," she said finally. "Colonel Briggs seems to think that women are only good for tending the wounded and sewing clothes. Many of us are trained in weapons, rescue, and more arduous things."

"You're capable of much more," Lawrence said, nodding. "The colonel needs to join the modern era."

"I think he needs to take his head out…" she paused, "…out of the nineteenth century."

Lawrence laughed and kissed his wife. "Maggie, you'll be home mornings and evenings. And it's two weeks until leave-out, when Olivia will be out of school. I believe we can trust our son not to get into any further trouble."

Tommy breathed a sigh of relief. He would have time for some adventures with Stumpy, who lived nearby.

CHAPTER

Saturday, 3 June 1944

The next morning, the post brought a letter from Aunt Kate, Margaret's sister. When Tommy came downstairs, Olivia was in the kitchen eating a bowl of porridge, and Margaret was talking with Lawrence while holding a blue envelope in the air.

"Kate wants me to come stay with her whilst she has her baby."

"And so?" said Tommy's father, looking up. "You can take Tommy and Olivia with you. She'll be happy to see them. It's been a year or two."

Margaret shook her head. "Her baby is actually imminent, but Kate is 'lying-in,' possibly for a week or more. And lying-in is so medieval! I was up and about a day after Olivia's birth. Tommy was even easier. She just thinks she needs me."

OPERATION OVERLORD | 33

"I am *not* going to stay in the boring countryside for weeks," Olivia declared. "Put me in a kennel."

Tommy, in the kitchen fixing himself a bowl of cornflakes, nodded. "That's not a bad idea. You would feel right at home."

Olivia flipped a spoonful of porridge at Tommy, which missed and landed in the sink. Tommy laughed as he poured milk into his cereal.

"That's the last of our milk ration until next week, Tommy," his mother said. "Just use a wee bit." Tommy obliged, even though barely damp cornflakes were not his favorite. "Same with the sugar, dear," she added.

"I've an idea," Olivia said. "I can lodge with Hazel whilst you're at Aunt Kate's. We've been talking about a stayover. And her mum is fine with the idea."

"I'll speak to Mrs. Finley," Margaret said, getting up from the table with an armload of dishes and utensils. "But what about Tommy?"

"Perhaps I can stay with Stumpy," he said, brightening. "We're planning to go camping this weekend."

The telephone rang. Lawrence went into the entry hall to answer. Tommy started to get up to listen, but his mother gave him a warning look that said clearly, "You know better."

Still, Tommy overheard a bit of his father's conversation. "The Mulberry harbours are in the

Channel, sir. The second batch is ready to go….I'll be there as soon as I can." He hung up the telephone, then dialed another number. "Good morning. This is Tommy's father. I was wondering—" He paused. "Ah. So your son has already asked." Another pause. "Well, thank you anyway."

Lawrence came back to the kitchen. Margaret, Olivia, and Tommy looked at him curiously and worriedly.

"Well, that tosses everything into a cocked hat," Lawrence said. He sat down at the kitchen table. "I've been called down to Southampton."

"Then it's on!" Tommy said. "The invasion!"

"I can't say," his father replied, "but it's because I don't know. Weather in the Channel is the worst it's been in years."

"Assuming Olivia will stay with Hazel, what do we do with Tommy?" Margaret wondered.

"I just spoke to Mrs. Ward. Stumpy's father is on duty in London. She and Stumpy are going to visit him as soon as term's over." He turned to Tommy. "I'm afraid your camping trip with Stumpy is off."

Margaret thought for a moment. "I suppose he could come with me to Aunt Kate's."

Tommy did not like the sound of that. He wanted to do something important, like organize his father's papers, or volunteer for the Air Raid Precautions group. "I could stay here and take care of the house," he said.

Mum and Dad shook their heads. Olivia smiled and said, "I've an idea. We'll put *you* in a kennel." Tommy had to laugh.

Lawrence thought for a moment. "I'll take Tommy with me to Southampton," he said. Noticing the expression on Margaret's face, he added, "It'll be as safe as we are here."

Olivia got up and took her bowl to the sink. She wiped a hand across her cheek with her back to the family. "It's…It's happening, isn't it."

Mum stood up, came to the sink, and put her arm around her daughter. "Your father won't be going over, dear," she said.

Olivia turned with tears in her eyes. "I know, I know. But it's this awful war. I'm so tired of it!" Margaret gave her daughter a squeeze. Dad rose from his chair and joined them, beckoning to Tommy, who joined them to make a family quartet.

"We've never been apart before," Margaret said.

"It won't be for very long, I hope," Lawrence said. "I think we'll have the Germans on the run."

The rest of the morning, the family spent packing: Olivia for her stayover with Hazel, Margaret for her trip to Bath to stay with her sister, Tommy for his adventure in Southampton. He stuffed the book *All-in Fighting* into his bag.

Tommy lugged his bag downstairs. He went out the front door and put it on the porch. His father poked his head out his office window. "We're leaving in an hour. Your mother is packing. We're taking her to the depot."

"I'm all packed up and ready to go, sir," Tommy said, saluting his father.

Lawrence saluted back with a grin. "Very good, cadet. You'll have time to say goodbye to Stumpy if you hurry."

Lawrence went back into his office. Tommy took *All-in Fighting* from his bag, tucked it in his jacket, and ran across the road to Stumpy's, a red brick, two-story house with a tiny vegetable garden in the side yard.

Stumpy saw him coming and hurried out the front door. "Are you in hot water for getting sent down?" he asked his friend.

"A bit," Tommy acknowledged. "Mum and Dad gave me a talking-to. But everything's changed. I'm going with Dad to Southampton. It's on!"

Stumpy's jaw dropped. "The invasion! When? Where are they going? Will you be helping?"

"Even Dad doesn't know yet. But it's soon. And I'll help if I'm needed." Tommy pulled *All-in Fighting* from his jacket. "I wanted to show you this. We can fight Hightower and his bullies."

Stumpy took the book and flipped through the pages, some with photographs, some with drawings of men fighting. Tommy and Stumpy spent the next hour poring over the book, practicing the wrist grabs, leg trips, and other maneuvers in the illustrations.

Mrs. Ward, a plump, cheerful woman, came out to the front. "You boys shouldn't be fighting," she said, shaking her finger at them.

"We're just practicing, Mum!" Stumpy said. "Getting ready to fight the Germans."

Mrs. Ward smiled. "Well, those Huns had better hope they don't run into you two," she said. "Tommy, your father called. You have to go home."

Tommy and Stumpy shook hands. "Take care, old chap," Tommy said. "Watch out for bullies at school."

Stumpy nodded. "I shall. And you take care. See you at fall term."

Tommy ran across the lane to his house, tucking *All-in Fighting* back into his bag. Mum and dad came out, each with a suitcase. Lawrence nodded at Tommy's bag. "Into the boot." Tommy and his father put the luggage into the rear of their car.

Olivia came out of the house, carrying a small suitcase. "Hazel's mum is coming to pick me up."

The family gathered to say their goodbyes. Olivia gave her brother a playful punch on the arm. "Try not to get into any more trouble," she said.

"You too," Tommy replied. "Resist any offers of black market eggs."

Olivia punched Tommy again, a bit harder. But she smiled.

Lawrence looked at his wristwatch. "The train leaves in an hour. We have to go." Margaret and Lawrence gave Olivia a hug, then got in the car. Tommy jumped into the back seat.

At the Winchester station, Tommy helped his dad unload Mum's scuffed leather bag. She seemed on the verge of crying, but she held it in. She kissed her husband and Tommy. "I do worry about the bombs. You'll be right in the thick of things."

"Southampton seems to be safe these last years," Lawrence said. "RAF and American raids on German airfields have been successful. The Nazis are about out of serviceable aircraft."

"I suppose that's a relief," Margaret said. "In truth, we're not all that safe here. That plane…right at the college…" Tommy noticed the worry lines on her face.

"I found out something about that," Lawrence said. "The pilot was deserting. He wanted to surrender. He was injured, but he survived. He's in hospital, under guard and under interrogation."

"We'll all be home before you know it." He beckoned to Tommy, who hopped into the passenger seat next to his father. Tommy turned to wave at his mum as they drove off.

On the drive to Southampton, Tommy's father was mostly quiet—thinking about the impending invasion, Tommy decided. They drove down St. Cross Road to the roundabout, then onto Otterbourne Road, past farms, grazing sheep and cattle, elm and larch trees lining the narrow road. They had to pull to the side below Chandler's Ford to allow a long convoy of military vehicles to pass. Tommy noticed American white stars in blue circles on the tanks aboard long tractor trailers. "The Yanks are coming," Tommy pointed out, remembering a long-ago song he'd heard on a scratchy record at his grandmother's house.

Lawrence smiled. "Over there, over there," he began singing in his off-key baritone. Tommy joined in, but neither of them could remember the words other than "over there," and "the Yanks are coming."

The Bournemouth Road had been damaged by bombing, and Lawrence had to slow to a crawl to navigate past workmen with picks and shovels. Despite his care, the Humber's front wheel hit a pothole, bouncing Tommy in his seat, and the motor sputtered to a stop. Lawrence hit the steering wheel with has hand, frustrated. "It's that coil wire!" he exclaimed. "We've got to move the car out of the roadway," he told Tommy.

Together, with Tommy steering and Lawrence pushing, they managed to get the vehicle to a spot under some trees. Lawrence raised the hood, beckoning to Tommy. "Come give me a hand," he said, ducking his head into the motor compartment.

Tommy climbed up on the running board to peer into the hot and smelly compartment. Lawrence held up a black wire with a bit of string tied to it. "This is the coil wire. The attachment is loose, and our mechanic can't get a new one due to the war shortages."

Tommy got a brief roadside education in automobile electrical circuitry. The distributor delivers electricity to the sparking plugs, which ignite the petrol that pumps into the engine's cylinders. The exploding petrol drives the pistons, which are connected to the crankshaft and rotate it. A gear on the crankshaft rotates a camshaft, which lifts and lowers valves to let petrol into the cylinders and exhaust gasses out. It also turns the gear on the distributor to send electricity to the sparking plugs. The car's battery provides electricity to the coil and then to the distributor, whilst the engine's generator charges the battery.

"It's a bit like the Allied forces," Lawrence said. "All working together to keep our country, our democracy, running to win this war." He pointed. "Snug that string that's tied round the coil wire to the top of the coil." Noticing the look on Tommy's face, Lawrence smiled.

"There's no electricity coming through. You won't get a shock."

Tommy leaned over the fender and into the engine compartment, the odors of petrol, hot oil, and unidentifiable things forcing him to breathe through his mouth. Lawrence pulled the string tight around the coil wire, wrapping and tying it tightly around the coil.

"That should do it," Lawrence said. Tommy hopped off the fender, and his father closed the hood. He took out a dirty rag from the car's boot, which Tommy recognized as a scrap of his old woolen shirt, and wiped his hands. He handed the rag to Tommy. "We'll wash up more thoroughly when we get there."

They got into the car. "Let's give it a try," Lawrence said, turning the key and pushing his foot down on the starter button. The motor fired right up. "Aha! Success!"

They stopped for lunch at a small pub in Boorley Green, then proceeded on. As they drew closer to Southampton, Tommy saw more and more signs of the impending invasion. Entire fields were lined with vehicles and row upon row of tents, with uniformed men moving about. A bit further on, they passed an airfield. Planes, many with the American star and fewer with the British red, white, and blue circle on their wings, were parked in rows on the grass. Lawrence pulled the car to the side of the road as convoys passed.

There were more and more bombed-out buildings. A single wall standing in a pile of rubble remained on the roadside, with a sign hanging by one hook: Lion & Cross—a drinking establishment.

The High Street was lined with bombed-out buildings. "A lot of people lost their lives here," Tommy's father said. The rubble and debris were stacked in neat piles along the roadway. Many other buildings were in repair. "But the attacks have stopped."

"We've almost won the war, then?" Tommy asked as they drove slowly through the potholed streets.

"We'll have won the war when the Germans surrender," Lawrence replied.

Arriving in Southampton, they turned onto Briton Street to Queen's Terrace, approaching a five-story stone-and-brick building with arched windows and black iron balconies. A few of the ground floor windows were boarded up, and stacks of sandbags surrounded the building entrance. Two soldiers stood guard at the door.

"The South Western Hotel," Lawrence said. "Also known as the HMS Shrapnel."

"HMS means his majesty's ship," Tommy said, puzzled. "But it's a building!"

Lawrence smiled. "Sometimes, we use HMS as a designation for Royal Naval offices on land. It's called a 'stone frigate.'"

Lawrence parked the Humber next to the curb on Canute Road. Across the street, workmen were repairing some damaged railroad tracks on the lower level. Lawrence and Tommy took out their bags and walked to the entrance. Tommy observed that his father held his grey briefcase close. The two soldiers saluted as they entered. Tommy, following his father, returned the salute. The soldiers returned his salute, smiling.

Inside the elegant, high-ceilinged, marble-floored lobby, Lawrence walked to a tall arched set of doors with a sign: *Operations Centre*. He knocked, and an armed guard opened the door. Lawrence turned to Tommy. "I'll just let them know I've arrived. Be back in a minute." He went inside. Tommy peered through the door to see a dozen men and women in uniform working on a giant map hung on the wall. The guard closed the door, and Tommy went back to the lobby to sit in one of the upholstered chairs.

Women wearing blue berets, skirts, and jackets, whom Tommy recognized as members of the Women's Royal Navy, called "Wrens," walked quickly in and out of the Operations Centre on urgent errands, carrying brown folders. There was excitement and tension in the hushed conversations of small groups of military men and men in suits. It was a feeling in the air, like a sound one could sense but not hear.

Tommy's father came out of the Operations Centre and sat in the chair next to Tommy. "A bit of excitement yesterday," he said, his voice in a low whisper. "Two local fishermen captured a German spy who had arrived by rowboat."

Tommy was captivated. "How did he get here? Rowing across the channel? How did they know he was a spy?"

Lawrence smiled. "Most likely he was dropped off by a German U-boat. I didn't hear the whole story, but he apparently aroused the locals' suspicions. The man tried to run, and the fishermen tackled him on the beach. One held him down whilst the other went for help." Lawrence stood up. "We'd better check in."

Tommy followed his father to the ornate front desk and rang the brass call bell. After a few seconds, an older, round-faced man, his tie slightly askew, came out from a room behind the desk. "We've been expecting you, Commander Collins," he said, handing him a key. "Your room is ready."

"Thank you, Mr. Smith," Lawrence replied. He looked down at Tommy. "You want your own key?" Tommy nodded, and Mr. Smith leaned over the desk and handed Tommy another room key.

"Come to help your father, have you?" he said, smiling. Tommy nodded.

Lawrence put the grey briefcase on the counter and took out a manila folder full of papers. Closing the latch, he handed the folder to Smith. "This must be kept in a secure place. But I will need access to it," he said.

Smith took the briefcase gingerly, as if afraid it might explode. "I'll put it in our safe in my office. There's a guard on duty at all times. It'll be safe as houses."

Lawrence pointed out the lobby window to a bombed-out building across the way. "'Safe as houses'? That expression might have outlived its usefulness," he said.

"Yes, well, er, that's true," Mr. Smith said, with an embarrassed chuckle. "That reminds me," he said, "the army ordnance team will be detonating an unexploded bomb this afternoon on Ocean Way. The police and ARP men will be out in force to keep people at a safe distance." Mr. Smith pulled a map from under the desk and put it on top. "It's here," he said, pointing, "near the old market."

Tommy's father glanced at the map and nodded. "We'll be sure to avoid the area."

Tommy stared at the map. "Can we go watch?" he asked his father.

Lawrence looked down at his son with one eyebrow raised. "No. And promise me you won't go anywhere near there."

Tommy had known what the answer would be, but he had to try. "I promise."

Mr. Smith rang the bell on his desk. "Hans will show you to your room."

A grey-haired man wearing a frayed tweed jacket and green vest came over to the desk. He nodded, smiling. "So? A young sailor und his father? I am Hans van Brugge." He held out his hands. "Let me carry your bags. I will show you upstairs." He took Lawrence's and Tommy's luggage. "Apart from some broken windows and shattered plaster, we've been fortunate to haf very little damage here." He shook his head angrily, muttering under his breath: "Those filthy Nazi swine."

Mr. Smith said, "Hans is from Holland. A refugee."

"Ya. Amsterdam. I saw what was coming. I came here a month before the Germans—the swine!—invaded my country."

Lawrence handed their two bags to van Brugge. They went upstairs, following the older man, who walked with a limp. He turned his head, smiling apologetically. "Forgive my slowness. I had an accident as a child. It never healed properly."

The room had two beds, a small deal table against the wall, a dresser with a mirror, and some slightly worn stuffed chairs. Tommy ran to a window with a narrow iron balcony that looked out over the harbor. He opened the window and stepped out, seeing warships of all sizes, from battleships and troop carriers to PT boats, filling the water from shore to shore. "That's more ships than I've ever seen!" he exclaimed.

His father stepped out next to him, and said, "That's more ships than anyone has ever seen in the history of the world." A submarine headed down the harbor and out to the channel. A gigantic, square-fronted ship backed slowly away from its dock accompanied by tiny tugboats hovering like baby ducks around a mother.

Lawrence pointed. "See those big, flat-fronted ships? They are called LSTs," he said. "Landing Ship, Tank. Those doors in the front are large enough for a Churchill or a Sherman tank to go through. The ships can ground themselves on beachheads to discharge equipment, then go back out to sea again."

He glanced up at the grey clouds gathering overhead. "There's more weather coming." Tommy knew his father was worried about conditions over the Channel that would delay the invasion.

Van Brugge put the bags down. "Shall I unpack for you, Commander?"

"We'll take care of it," Lawrence replied. "Thank you." He put his hand into his jacket and took out his wallet.

Van Brugge shook his head. "No, no. No gratuity. Your service to my adopted country is payment enough." He smiled and backed out the door, closing it.

Lawrence and Tommy came indoors and unpacked their bags. A cold wind blew in the open window, and rain followed.

"I hope you brought your books. There's not much to do elsewise," Lawrence said. "I'll be in meetings downstairs most of the day."

Tommy reached into his bag and took out his books: *The Wizard of Oz* and *Treasure Island*. He was careful to leave *All-in Fighting* under a shirt at the bottom. "I'm sure I'll keep myself occupied," Tommy said.

Lawrence came over, reached into Tommy's bag, and took out *All-in Fighting*. Tommy blushed and looked away. "You can always practice with this," his father said, frowning. "Did you imagine I wouldn't notice it was gone from my bookshelf?"

"I'm sorry, Dad," Tommy said, looking down at the floor, out the window, anywhere but into his father's blue eyes. "After my run-in with Hightower, I thought I should learn how to defend myself."

Lawrence nodded. "I understand. But you took the book without my permission. You could have asked me."

"I'm sorry," Tommy said again.

"Here's the thing: this book was written to show how to defend yourself against someone who might intend to do you real harm, to kill you." Lawrence waved the book. "Perhaps some of the instructions might be useful for schoolyard bullies. Getting free from someone who grabs your wrists, that kind of thing. But much of it is…" he hesitated, "…is dangerous." He tilted up Tommy's downcast head and looked in his eyes. "Understand?"

"Yes, sir," Tommy said.

"I can trust your good judgement then?"

"Yes, sir."

Lawrence went to the tiny table, took a manila folder from his briefcase, and tucked it under his arm. Then he put on his cap. "I'll be back for supper. There's good food in the restaurant downstairs, depending on rationing. Or we could go out for fish and chips."

"Fish and chips!" Tommy replied, smiling hopefully.

Tommy spent the next half-hour practicing the moves from the book, showing an imaginary Hightower and his bullies what-for. Then the bullies became Nazis, and Tommy gave them a right whipping.

Tommy soon became bored fighting with pretend villains. He flopped on the bed and opened *The Wizard of Oz*, but he wasn't in the mood for tin men or scarecrows. Outside, the rain had stopped, a few feeble rays of afternoon sunshine breaking through the blanket of clouds outside. He could hear the ships' horns, the roar of lorry motors, and the shouts of men at the work of loading vehicles and equipment. Tommy wanted to go down to the harbor to see the preparations for the greatest invasion in all of history. He put on his jacket and went out, careful to lock the room door behind him.

Mr. Smith wasn't at the front desk, and the lobby was almost empty. Everyone was at a meeting, Tommy supposed. Van Brugge came down the hallway, nodding and smiling. "Off on an adventure?"

"Just going to have a look around," Tommy said.

"Be careful," van Brugge said. "There are falling-down buildings, dangerous craters, unexploded bombs yet in some areas. Stay on the pavements." He shook his head angrily. "Filthy swine," he muttered.

Tommy walked down Canute Road to Ocean Way, thinking he might see a bit of the bomb detonation. But he'd promised his father, and besides, there were police and barricades at the intersection. He turned left, heading for the harbor, where a thousand ships were loading for the invasion. The closer he got to the docks, the more bombed buildings, uprooted trees, and giant holes in the roadway he saw. The sun still shone feebly, but dark clouds were moving in from the west.

He walked past a bombed shop with only two of its walls left standing and piles of stone and rubble visible through the glassless front windows. A broken sign over the door read only, *ey's Radios and Gramophones.* Tommy heard a noise from inside. Someone was opening cabinets, moving things around. Then a young voice, a girl's voice: "*Er moet hier ergens iemand zijn…*"

Tommy had heard Hitler's ranting on the wireless at home. This person was speaking German. *Another spy, like the one captured at the beach,* he thought. Then in accented English, he heard, "It's just a condenser."

Up to no good, Tommy was sure of it. He stepped carefully over the potholes next to the shop front, edged up against the wall, and peered inside. A girl with her back to him was on her knees on the floor of the shop. She was looking through a box and tossing out bits of things that looked like radio parts: a coil of copper wire, broken tubes, and switches.

Tommy's first thought was to find a police constable. But what if she escaped before he could locate one? Then he decided he would stop her himself. She was just a girl, at any rate. And he'd been practicing his all-in fighting.

"Stop, Nazi. Surrender!" Tommy said in his bravest voice.

The girl leapt to her feet and turned to face him. "I am not a Nazi," she said in her German-sounding accent. "Who are you?"

Tommy was expecting more guilty behavior. "Never mind who I am," he said. "I'm turning you in to the authorities."

The girl bent down to retrieve a dirty cloth bag then put the strap over her shoulder. She straightened up and stepped toward him, and Tommy noticed she was wearing pants. She had dark brown hair down to her neck, brown eyes, and a smudge of dirt on her chin. She was just about Tommy's height. Despite his confidence in his training, Tommy took a step back. He looked up and down the street for a uniform. None was in sight.

"You are a Nazi spy!"

The girl laughed. Not what Tommy expected. "And you are going to arrest me?"

Tommy lowered his voice. "Just come along quietly."

The girl laughed again. She held out her arms. "Let us go then."

Tommy remembered the wrist grab from the book. He took hold of the girl's left wrist with his right and started to twist it. The next thing he knew, he was on his back, a brick poking painfully into his shoulder.

The girl stepped next to him and held out her hand to help him up. "Here. You can try again." Tommy waved her hand away and got to his feet. "I don't want to hurt you," he said.

"Oh, that is good. I was worried."

Tommy moved quickly behind her, grabbing her arms. His reward was a hard stomp on his foot and a kick to his shin. He tripped, fell backwards, and landed on his bum. "Ow!" He said, rubbing his leg.

"What's all this, then?" a gruff voice said. Tommy looked up to see a tall, ruddy-cheeked man with thinning blond hair standing at the shop entrance. "Are you all right, Annike?"

"I am fine, Mr. Woolsey," the girl replied.

Tommy got up slowly, looking down at the ground to see the rest of the ruined sign: *Wools*.

"Is this ruffian bothering you?" Mr. Woolsey asked, pointing at Tommy with a frown.

"Oh, no," the girl replied. "This *jongen*...this boy thinks I am a Nazi engaged in sabotage."

"You were speaking German!" Tommy said.

"You *dom hoofd*—" she paused, "you dumb head!"

Mr. Woolsey chuckled, running his hands over his hair. "That's a good one, that is." He looked at Tommy again. Tommy looked down at the ground. "You're way off here. Annike here is from Holland, a guest of the British government. This is—or was—my shop, before the Jerries bombed it. The family and I were away, or we would have been under all this," he added. "Annike has my permission to be here." He shook his head. "Even though I warned her it might be dangerous. She's a stubborn lass."

Tommy had to admit his error. He held out his hand to Annike. "Tommy Collins. I apologize, Annike." Once more trying to salvage his judgement, he added. "But you do have an accent."

Annike shook her head, her hair swishing around. "No, *you* have an accent!"

Mr. Woolsey laughed. "You are both right, I think."

Annike started to reach for Tommy's hand then stopped. "You aren't going to throw me over your shoulder or something like that?"

Tommy smiled despite his recent humiliation. "No. A good handshake is all."

"Annike Meier." She nodded, not smiling.

"Tommy Collins." He shook her hand. "You're not going to kick me again, are you?"

Annike shook her head. "Not unless you try to arrest me for spying."

Mr. Woolsey patted Annike on the back. "All's well, then." To Tommy, he asked, "Do you live in town, Master Collins?"

"No, sir. My father's in the Navy. He's here…for meetings," he said, not willing to reveal too much.

"Ah, the invasion, then," Mr. Woolsey nodded. "It's finally on, is it?"

Tommy shrugged. "My dad says, 'Those who know, don't say—'"

"And those who say, don't know," Mr. Woolsey finished. "Well, you're a good lad, Master Collins. I pray for us all." He looked up at the sky. "It's going to rain again," he said. "We'd all better get undercover." Rain started to patter down as if in answer. Mr. Woolsey waved and headed back down the street.

"I'd better get back," Tommy said. "Dad will be looking for me soon."

"Do not be so quick to judge," Annike said.

Tommy, still feeling on the outs, walked away. He stopped and turned, wanting to ask the girl what she was doing. But she had vanished.

Lawrence was waiting for Tommy in the hotel lobby. The rain had started in earnest, and Tommy was soaking wet. His dad raised an eyebrow. "Taking a bath?"

Tommy smiled. "I was just doing a bit of exploring," he said. "I didn't go near the bomb crew."

"Go upstairs, dry yourself off, and change. It's no good going out to eat. We'll have supper here."

Despite the wartime rationing, the hotel had some excellent food, Tommy decided. A slice of roast beef, peas, and carrots—which Tommy picked at—a baked potato with oleomargarine, not butter, unfortunately, and a fair chocolate pudding for dessert. Tommy wiped the last bit of pudding off his chin and licked his finger. His dad handed him his otherwise unused napkin.

"How long can we stay here?" Tommy asked, cleaning his chocolaty fingers with the napkin.

Lawrence smiled. "You prefer the meals here to the ones at home? You'd better not say that to your mother."

Tommy smiled, blushing a little. "Well, it is a nice change."

"So, tell me how you got soaking wet."

Tommy told his father about his explorations. "I was walking down the road when I heard someone rummaging around in a radio shop. I thought it might have been spies or saboteurs. It was…someone looking for stuff." He neglected to mention that it was a girl who outfought him.

Lawrence drank the last of his tea and got up from the table. "Time for young saboteur-catchers to go to bed."

In their room, Lawrence took some papers out of his briefcase. Tommy saw the word BIGOT in red ink stamped on the pages. "What does that stand for, dad?"

"British Invasion of German Occupied Territories," his father answered. "And no, you may not look at them. They are classified Most Secret, above Top Secret." He pointed to the bed. "Go to bed. I'll keep the light low."

Tommy began to put on his pajamas. His father noted a reddish bruise on his shoulder. "How'd you get that welt?"

"Uhh, I tripped on some rubble," Tommy said, not quite a lie. "It doesn't hurt." He jumped into bed, grabbing *All-in Fighting* to read. He thought he must have missed a lesson; otherwise, he was sure he could have bested that girl. She was just a girl, after all. Tommy fell asleep with the open book on his chest.

CHAPTER

Sunday, 4 June 1944

A clap of thunder startled Tommy into wakefulness. His father, already wearing his dress blues, was stuffing papers into his briefcase.

"Since it's pouring out, you'll have nothing to do but get into trouble here," he said. "But I found you some useful employ." He pointed to a small table near the door. "There's tea and toast. Wash up, brush your teeth, eat a bit, get dressed, and we'll go. And don't forget to make your bed. We've no maid service."

Tommy yawned, stretched, and tossed off the bedcovers. "What will I be doing? Where are we going?"

"Southwick House. You'll find out when we get there." His father put his finger to his lips. "Tell no one."

Tommy smiled. Whom would he tell, anyway?

One can see Southwick house for a mile before one arrives. A dark stone, three-story mansion in the

Georgian style, it sits atop a hill with a commanding view to the south and Portsmouth harbor, where the thousand ships were docked and awaiting orders—orders that would come from here. Today, though, with the rain and low clouds, it was hard to see even to the bottom of the hill.

As Tommy and his dad drove up the graveled road, they passed ten or more dun-grey and olive-green sedans, lorries, troop transports, and even an American tank, which Tommy thought must be a Sherman. A steel gate blocked the road as they neared the house, and a guard in an American soldier's uniform came out. Lawrence showed him his pass, the guard saluted, and the gate opened.

On the grounds in front of the house were a dozen olive-green tents and grey corrugated steel huts. Lawrence parked and they went in.

The entrance to Southwick House was like a temple or a church. A large round entry hall rose three stories high, with a domed glass ceiling. Paintings on the sides of the dome were scenes from history or mythology.

Tommy peered into an open door. The high-ceilinged room looked like a library, except all the bookshelves were empty. Logs hissed in the fireplace. A giant floor-to-ceiling map of the European coastline filled a wall, with smaller maps on the tables. Hurrying Wrens carrying clipboards and colored markers moved wheeled ladders from place to place along the map-covered walls. Ten or more men and women in uniform worked at tables, talking quietly. Telephone cables crisscrossed the wooden floor.

Tommy looked at a map on a table. Thousands of tiny model ships were on the map off the coast of France. Sections of the coast were lettered: Juno, Sword, Arromanches, Omaha, Utah, each marked with British, Canadian, and American flags on them. A uniformed Wren wearing headphones listened then used a long stick to move the tiny ships on the map, pushing them to the part of the map close to France.

As he came out of the room, Tommy turned to see his father heading to a broad hallway. He hurried to catch up to him. Several doors led off to the sides, and a broad staircase with wrought-iron balusters was crowded with men and women in uniform hurrying up and down.

Tommy's father took his arm. "I found some useful work for you," he said. They crossed the hall to a door marked Radio. Inside a long, narrow room were a dozen men and women, all in uniform, wearing black earphones and sitting at wireless units. They were writing swiftly, stuffing the papers into brown folders, and waving their hands in the air. Other men and women wearing red armbands hurried to the waving hands, took the folders, and hurried off.

Lawrence walked across the room to a desk in the corner. Tommy followed his father, keeping out of the rushing messengers' way. A tall, thin man wearing Army kit stood up as they approached. He held out his hand. "Commander Collins," he said.

Lawrence shook his hand. "Tommy, meet Lieutenant Michael Shaffer, Royal Signals. He'll be your superior officer."

Tommy opened his mouth, closed it again. "Superior...What?"

"I had to call in a favor, but whilst I'm busy, you will be doing the job of the men and women in red armbands. They're taking messages to the appropriate recipients."

Lieutenant Shaffer held out his hand, and Tommy shook it. "Pleased to meet you, sir."

"Likewise," the lieutenant said. He picked up a red armband and fastened it to Tommy's shirtsleeve. "It'll take you a bit to get up to speed, but I'm sure you'll catch on. Your father tells me you're a quick study."

Tommy looked down at his armband and grinned with pride. He was contributing to the war effort. He wasn't just some anonymous boy, but a soldier—almost. He saluted Lieutenant Shaffer. "I shall do my best."

The lieutenant pointed to a chair next to the desk. "Have a sit. I'll explain your duties."

Lawrence patted Tommy on his shoulder. "I'm off. Be back at mealtime. We'll eat in the canteen." He pointed out the window to a long greenish-brown tent where men and women were going in and out with trays.

The task wasn't hard. When a radio operator raised a hand, Tommy would dash to the radio desk. The operator would hand him a large yellow envelope, and Tommy was to read the writing in red on the back, which noted a room number. As fast as he could, Tommy was to deliver the envelope to the appropriate room.

"Numbers one through nine are all on the ground floor," the lieutenant explained. "Ten to twenties are on the first floor. The top floor is billets. You won't be going there." He pointed at a paper on his desk. "And you're only to read the room number. Open the envelope, and we might think you're a spy." He said this last with a smile, but Tommy nodded seriously. He thought about Annike.

Tommy spent the rest of the morning busier than he'd ever been. He hurried between the aisles of radio operators, taking folders and rushing out to find the correct door. Tommy had to dodge other runners going up and downstairs. By lunchtime, he was tired. He flopped down in the chair across from Lieutenant Shaffer.

A few minutes later, his father entered the radio room. "Time for a bite, I'd say."

Tommy now realized he was very hungry. He stood up. "Permission to leave, sir?" he asked, saluting the lieutenant.

"Permission granted," Lieutenant Shaffer replied, saluting.

Tommy and his father went outside to the large canteen tent, where soldiers, sailors, and airmen were lining up. The rain had let up, but a cold wind blew across the lawn, which was deeply rutted and torn from the passage of tanks and other vehicles. Clouds were forming overhead.

Lawrence looked up, frowning. "Not optimal, I'd say."

"So we still don't know if it's on then?" Tommy asked.

"No. The Royal Air Force weatherman, Group Captain Stagg, has been providing reports hourly, and I know there's a big meeting this afternoon. Perhaps they'll make a decision."

They both turned at the noise of vehicles coming up the graveled drive. In the lead was a gleaming black-and-green Rolls-Royce limousine, followed by a dark-green American car with a white star on its rear doors, several military vehicles, and armored vehicles with gunners atop them.

As the caravan drew closer, Tommy spotted the Union Jack flag mounted on the front and a red placard with four gold stars on it. The Rolls pulled to a stop at the main entrance to Southwick House.

Instantly every man and woman on the lawn put down their trays of food and snapped to attention. Tommy's father did likewise, and Tommy followed suit.

A plump, red-faced man in a dark-blue military uniform opened the rear door and stepped out before a uniformed sergeant could reach the handle.

"It's Winnie himself," his father said. Winston Churchill, the British prime minister, puffed on his cigar as he walked up the stairs to the entrance. "He's wearing his Air Commodore uniform." Tommy looked puzzled, and his father explained, "He served in the last war."

Behind the Rolls, the American car arrived. A woman driver in an American military uniform leapt out and opened the rear door. A tall, thin, balding man in an Army uniform stepped out and put his peaked cap on as he straightened up. The four gold stars on his shoulders shone in the dim sunlight.

"General Eisenhower," Lawrence said unnecessarily. Tommy had seen his picture in the newspapers: the supreme commander of the Allied forces.

The other side door of the Rolls opened, and a short, wiry man in a British Army uniform with a pencil-thin grey moustache and a black beret, stepped out. He walked rapidly to catch up with Eisenhower and Churchill, who were already near the entrance.

"That's Monty," Tommy said. "Field Marshal General Bernard Montgomery," he corrected himself.

All the forty or so military men and women on the green saluted, as did Tommy and his dad. General Eisenhower turned at the top of the steps and returned the salute. Churchill doffed his hat. Monty went inside without looking back.

"We'd better hurry and eat," Tommy said. "You'll be wanted at the meeting."

His dad chuckled. "Oh no, not me. I'm just a small cog in this giant wheel. My part is all but done, thanks to the prime minister's clever idea."

"What was that?" Tommy asked as they returned to the tent to get their food.

"I was working on something called Mulberry Harbours. They're floating docks, a method of getting men and equipment on shore where there's no usable harbor."

They sat down at an otherwise empty table. Lawrence opened the folder he always carried to show Tommy a photograph. "You've seen these in the harbor."

To Tommy they looked like giant concrete blocks. "They float?"

Lawrence nodded. "Concrete floats if there's enough air in it. These docks connect our ships to the shore, allowing vehicles to drive to the beaches." He tucked the photograph back into the folder. "Our intelligence service has been using captured German spies to pass along rumors of an invasion planned for several places."

"So we won't be landing where they expect us," Tommy said, remembering from newspaper photographs of the docks and piers at the French port. He'd heard the rumors of the invasion happening at a half-dozen locations, including Norway and Spain, but he knew that many of these stories were merely to confuse the enemy.

Lawrence shrugged. "It depends. Maybe we will, maybe we won't. Either way, we will be prepared."

Lunch meant more Spam, Tommy was sorry to see, but also a fresh garden salad and, of all things, vanilla ice cream. Putting their plates and utensils in grey metal containers, Tommy and his dad returned to work.

Later that afternoon, Lawrence entered the radio room to find Tommy curled up on a couch asleep, despite the noise and bustle around him.

Lieutenant Shaffer came over, pushing his glasses up on his nose. "I'm afraid I've worn him out, sir. But he's a hard worker."

"Thanks for keeping him occupied, lieutenant," Lawrence said. "I'm glad he was of some help."

Lawrence nudged Tommy awake. He sat up and yawned. "Hullo, Dad," he said. "Is there more to do?"

"Not now. We can go back to the HMS Shrapnel and have some tea and biscuits."

Tommy said goodbye to Lieutenant Shaffer, and he and his father got in the Humber. They went slowly back to the South West Hotel, avoiding potholes so as not to dislodge the coil wire. More and more lorries, tanks, and half-tracks occupied the road, all heading to the port. The rain began again, with the Humber's feeble wipers pushing the drops around on the windscreen.

Tommy and his father arrived at the hotel and went up to their room. His father went into the bathroom and came out a few minutes later in a robe. He got into battle dress: boots, leggings, brown pants, and shirt. "There's not much hot water, but you ought to bathe," he told Tommy.

Tommy dressed after his lukewarm shower and found his father looking through folders in his suitcase. "Did you poke about in my papers?" he asked sternly.

"No, Dad. I'd never do that," Tommy replied, although that hadn't always been true. Back home, he'd looked at the pictures and documents on his father's desk. But not here.

"Hmmm. There's nothing missing, but…" His father scratched his head. "All right. I might be overcautious. Let's go downstairs."

Lawrence approached Mr. Smith at the front desk. "Has anyone been in our rooms?"

Mr. Smith shook his head. "No, no, Commander. I gave strict orders to the staff. No one is allowed in." He reached down behind the desk and took out a slip of red paper. "There's a message for you, sir. Delivered by courier."

Lawrence read the message, making a wry face. "I have to go back to Southwick now." He said to Tommy, "You'll be by yourself. The weather will be frightful. Don't go out and get soaked."

"Of course, Dad," Tommy said, and he meant it when he said it. "Is it on then?" he asked in a low voice, looking around the lobby for anyone who might be listening.

His father shook his head. "You know better than to ask." Lawrence gave Tommy a quick hug and a handshake, then spoke to Mr. Smith about supper for his son.

"I'll see that the lad is well-fed, sir," Mr. Smith said. As Lawrence went out, Mr. Smith came out from behind the desk to lead Tommy to a chair. "How about a nice cuppa?" he asked. Tommy nodded.

As Tommy sipped his tea and devoured his third chocolate biscuit, van Brugge came into the lobby carrying a broom and dustpan. He smiled at Tommy. "Zo, you have been helping your father, I hear."

Tommy nodded. "But I'm not allowed to talk about it," he said.

Van Brugge chuckled. "Of course, of course. All very top-secret, hush-hush," he said. "Well, I hope the invasion is soon. I want my country back." He held up a broom and dustpan. "I must finish my work," he said. "Keep yourself safe."

"Thank you," Tommy replied. He got up from the table and went back to the room. He thought again about reading or practicing his fighting skills then wandered over to the window to look out at the harbor. A large, grey ship with a red cross on its hull was sailing down the harbor and out to sea. Clouds were wafting overhead with faint afternoon sunlight shining through.

Sit in the room or explore? Not a difficult decision for a twelve-year-old boy in Southampton on the cusp of the greatest military invasion in history. It was the biggest thing that had ever happened in his young life. He'd promised his father not to get wet, so he decided he'd come back if it started to rain.

Tommy put on his jacket then went downstairs and out the hotel's front door. After ten minutes watching the military vehicles drive up and down Canute Road and hearing the ship horns and traffic, he decided to go down to the docks to see better.

Tommy sat on a concrete pier at the edge of the docks at the harbor watching the dozens of men and women directing the loading of armored vehicles and jeeps, some with cannons mounted atop them. As evening drew near, floodlights came on, making everything as bright as day.

A convoy of heavy lorries with the American five-pointed star on their doors drove slowly down the pier towards a ramp that led to the cavernous doors of an LST. The lorries all had to make sharp turns so they could back into the hold.

It was getting dark. The wind blew colder. Tommy got up and walked back to the street leading to the hotel. Although there had been no recent Luftwaffe attacks, blackout conditions were still in effect. The few people on the street were using their torches to light the way.

Before he realized it, Tommy had taken a detour to pass by the ruins of Mr. Woolsey's shop. He saw a flash of light from inside and heard Annike's voice: "Aha. *Gevonden!*" There was a clatter of stones, and Annike came out with her white bag over her shoulder. She looked up to see Tommy, shining her torch beam in his face. "Master Collins! Still hunting spies?"

Tommy laughed despite the fact that the joke was on him. "Not this time," he said. "Why are you collecting old radio parts?"

Annike lowered her torch and held up a battered cardboard box. "I am making a wireless. I found what I needed. Now I have to finish putting it together."

"Why are you making a wireless?" Tommy asked.

Annike tucked the torch under her arm and opened the box. Inside were two glass cylinders Tommy recognized as radio tubes. Annike beckoned. "Come. I will show you. It's almost time for Shabbat dinner."

"A what?" Tommy hurried to catch up to Annike as she strode quickly up the street.

It had begun to rain in earnest as Tommy and Annike turned off the street onto a row of older houses with small front yards.

"We are getting soaked!" Annike cried. "Hurry!"

Tommy and Annike ran up the pitch-dark street. She opened the front gate of a small two-story house with a brick-fronted ground floor and a Tudor wood-and-plaster upper story, and the two dashed up the walk. Blackout curtains covered all the windows.

As the two approached the front door, it opened. A tall, angular woman wearing a headscarf stepped out. "Annike, dear. I was beginning to worry. How was your search? And who is this young man?"

"This is Tommy," Annike replied. "He's chasing spies." She held up her bag. "And now I have the tubes!"

She beckoned to them. "Come in, dears. You're getting drenched out here."

Annike and Tommy entered, dripping wet and shivering from the cold. Annike started up the narrow stairs. "I am going to change my clothes."

The woman held out her hand to Tommy. "You can call me Delilah."

Tommy shook her hand. "My name is Tommy."

Delilah nodded. "Annike has spoken of you." She smiled, making Tommy wonder what Annike said.

An older man with a grey beard, wearing a skullcap and a white shawl around his neck, came over and shook Tommy's hand. "Welcome, lad. I am Rabbi Stein," he said. "Let's get you some dry clothes as well."

He beckoned, and a boy a few years older than Tommy, with dark brown hair and a bucktoothed grin, came over. "Hi. I'm Lev. Come on upstairs." Tommy walked past the dining room, passing a candlelit table.

Upstairs, Lev pointed to a tiny bathroom, where Tommy took off his wet clothes and dried himself off with a large, white, well-worn towel. The boy opened the door a crack and handed in a faded green shirt and a pair of pants. The shirtsleeves came down over his hands, and Tommy had to hold the pants up. The door opened a crack again, and Lev's arm reached in, holding a belt. Tommy put it on.

Tommy came downstairs a few minutes later. Annike, in dry clothes, Lev, and Delilah were sitting around the table. Rabbi Stein nodded, "Join us. We're about to observe our Sabbath—a little later than usual, due to your late arrival." He finished with a smile.

Tommy sat down, still not understanding. Rabbi Stein began: "*Baruch hatah Adonai...*"

It wasn't German, Tommy realized. There were small books at each place on the table written in a language he'd never seen before. The others joined in, their heads lowered. Tommy bowed his head.

"We thank Adonai for our rescue and our welcome in this great land," Rabbi Stein said. "We pray to Him to care for and guide others who still remain in bondage. May they, like our ancestors in the time of Moses, soon find freedom."

"*Amen,*" everyone said together.

Delilah got up from the table. "And now it's time to eat. Lev, Annike, come help me serve."

Tommy had never seen food like this. Delilah had, despite wartime rationing, prepared a delicious meal: a shiny-crust bread tied in knots, called *challah,* a stew of potatoes, yams, onions and carrots with a little bit of beef, and for dessert, dark biscuits called macaroons. Lev held up a bottle, looking over at Delilah. She nodded, and the boy poured Tommy a small glass of a sweet red wine that reminded him of grape soda.

After dinner, the group got up and moved into the living room, which had been converted to a bed-sitting room. Annike pointed to a fold-out couch. "That is my bed," she told Tommy. She walked out of the room. "Delilah! I will help you clean up!"

"Annike doesn't take up much room," Delilah told Tommy. "The poor dear came to us with just a tiny suitcase."

"Why is Annike here?" Tommy asked. "Where are her parents?"

Lev walked over to Tommy. "I will explain." Lev sat in a narrow chair, and Tommy on a corner of the couch. "Annike was part of something called Kindertransport. It was planned by rescue organizations before Germany started the war," Lev said. "They managed to save thousands of children, even infants, from Poland, Germany, Czechoslovakia, and the Netherlands, sending them to safety before the outbreak of war in 1939. Many, like Annike, were Jewish. The children had to leave their parents behind, go to a country where they didn't speak the language, and live with strangers without knowing if they'd ever see their families again."

Tommy was silent. He couldn't imagine being sent away from his family to live in a strange country. He again felt guilty for his suspicions and thought about apologizing.

Annike came into the living room, carrying a battered and wrinkled manila folder. She patted the seat. She sat on the couch, patting the seat beside her. "Come here," she said. "I have some pictures." She opened the folder and took out a small stack of black-and-white photographs.

Tommy sat. "I want to say I'm sorry—" he began.

Annike interrupted him, waving her hand. "For thinking I was a Nazi? Pfft." She made a noise. "I thought you were a stupid boy." She took a faded photograph from the folder. "This is my house in Amsterdam," Annike said. It was a tall, narrow, four-story brick house. Its front wall had stone steps leading to a peak. A sign on the front read Radio Winkel. "That's my father's store," Annike said, then sighed. "Or it was, before the Nazis. They made him close it because Dutch people were not to be trusted with radios. And because we were Jewish."

Another photograph showed a tall, blond man with a beard; a short, smiling woman; and a young girl and boy. "My family. That's me, my brother Josef, *mijn moeder en vader.*"

Delilah came over and sat on the arm of the couch. "Thomas, you should know, Annike hasn't heard from her family in almost four years," Delilah said. "But she's very determined to try."

Annike jumped up from the couch and held out her hand. "I will show you how I am going to talk to my family." Tommy took her hand, and she yanked him up. "Come."

Tommy followed Annike through the house into the kitchen and out the rear door. "Be careful," Annike said. "It's dark and you cannot see the way."

Tommy's eyes adjusted to the blackout darkness. He followed Annike to a small, peaked-roof, windowless wooden shed at the rear of the property. It was still raining, but not as hard as before. Annike opened the shed door, and they went in. It was even darker inside. She closed the door and turned on the light, a single yellow bulb hanging over a wooden workbench.

Tommy walked over to the bench, picking up a black-handled screwdriver-like tool sitting in a rusty iron cradle. "That's my soldering iron," Annike said. She pointed to a scattered pile of parts: copper wires wound around a cardboard cylinder, a wooden board with more wires attached to it.

"I have been making a radio, with help from Mr. Woolsey, because I made a promise to my father," Annike said. "I would try to contact him on my birthday."

"When is your birthday?" Tommy asked.

"The sixth of June."

"That's Tuesday!" Tommy exclaimed.

"That's why I am hurrying," Annike replied. "My parents have left Holland and I don't know where they are, or if they will have a wireless. If they can, they will listen for me."

"Where could they go?" Tommy asked. "All of Europe is occupied."

"Sweden," Annike said. "It is a neutral country, no Germans. They were arranging to take a boat, a fishing boat, to a tiny town in Norway and then across to Sweden."

"You know how to make a radio?"

"Do you think a girl is not able to do such a thing?" Annike sounded insulted. "My father owned a radio shop. I learned how to repair radios and gramophones for his customers."

Tommy realized that he'd been wrong in more than one way. "I'm sorry, Annike. I thought you were a saboteur."

"And you thought you were a better fighter," she said.

"I'm a good fighter!" Tommy replied. Now it was his turn to feel insulted. "You just surprised me."

"A good fighter would not be surprised," Annike said.

Tommy was angry. He opened the door to go out. "You're letting the light out!" Annike yelled at him. "The blackout!"

Tommy slammed the shed door and went back to the house, stubbing his toe on a rock he failed to notice.

Inside, Rabbi Stein was putting on his coat. "I was just coming to look for you. We called your hotel. Your father was worried. I will take you home."

Tommy was still mad. "I can find my way back," he said.

"No, no. It is too dangerous. You have no torch to light your way. And you'll get soaked again. I insist." The rabbi had Tommy's wet clothes wrapped up in newspaper.

Tommy got into the passenger seat of an ancient black sedan, which started with a rattle. The headlamps were painted black, with only tiny unpainted slits of light to show the way. Rabbi Stein drove carefully through the pitch-dark streets, avoiding the occasional piles of broken stone. The windscreen wipers were just able to keep up with the rain, which was coming down harder than ever, adding to Tommy's gloom.

Now the invasion was off. His father's work would be for nothing, all those ships, men, and equipment already at sea or sitting in the harbor would be idled for who knew how long. And he'd been wrong about that Dutch girl. But she was very annoying.

And his father would be waiting for him.

Sure enough, when the car wheezed up to the curb in front of the hotel, Tommy's father was standing under the portico talking to the sentry.

"Thank you, Mr. Stein," Tommy said as he opened the car door.

"Don't forget your clothes," Rabbi Stein said, pointing with his thumb to the rear seat. "And you are welcome at our house any time, lad."

Tommy reached over the seat to retrieve his clothes wrapped in newspaper. He got out and walked to the hotel entrance, the longest short walk he could remember. He was barely able to look at his father, who stood with his hands on his hips.

"We'll talk inside," he said, nodding to the sentry as they went in.

Upstairs in their room, Lawrence pulled the blackout curtains over the windows then turned on the light. He pointed to a chair. "Sit." Tommy sat, looking down at the floor. "You disobeyed me," he said.

"No, I didn't," Tommy protested. "You said, 'Don't go out and get soaked.' It wasn't raining when I went out."

Despite his anger, Lawrence smiled. "With a defense like that, you might have a career as a barrister, young man." He sat down across from his son. "Fortunately for you, when I got back there was a message at the desk from a Mrs. Stein telling me where you were, or I'd have been at my wit's end. What on earth possessed you, son?"

Tommy, remembering his parents' adage "the truth is always best," told his father about going to the docks to watch the invasion preparations and running into Annike, who invited him to her house. He left out the part about his disastrous fight with her but told his father about Kindertransport.

Lawrence got up. "Time for bed. We're in meetings here tomorrow. The prime minister, Generals Eisenhower and Montgomery, and a lot of brass. Still hoping the weather will be in our favor. You will keep yourself gainfully employed. Mr. Smith has some jobs for you. No more hunting for spies or saboteurs. Understood?"

"Yes, sir," Tommy replied, meaning it.

CHAPTER 7

Monday, 5 June 1944

Tommy spent the morning helping van Brugge clean up rubbish from a hotel outbuilding. The Dutchman gave him a pair of gloves, which helped somewhat, but Tommy still got a splinter in his hand, dirt on his face, and gravel in his shoes. This was supposed to be punishment, but Tommy found the work a bit enjoyable. He was building up his strength to be a better fighter. Tommy wiped the sweat off his forehead with his sleeve.

"You work good, young man," van Brugge said, smiling. "Your father will be happy." He nodded his head towards the hotel. "They are in meetings in there. The invasion will be soon, I think."

Tommy shrugged. "My father doesn't know. I don't think anyone does. It's the weather."

Van Brugge nodded. "I hope it happens soon. People are suffering." He turned away, wiping his cheeks.

Perhaps van Brugge was worried about his family. Like Annike.

By noon, Tommy was tired and hungry. Van Brugge had gone elsewhere, so Tommy went up to the room and took another lukewarm shower. He had a few shillings and thought he'd go find the fish and chips place his father had mentioned.

It was still overcast but not actually raining. The streets were busy: it was market day. Women and men were visiting shops, stopping by the stalls with piles of fresh vegetables, cartons of eggs, and even some fruit. The butcher's shop had a line outside. A handwritten sign in the window read Fresh pork—limited quantity.

Tommy asked a woman carrying a shopping bag for directions to the fish and chips shop. She pointed up the street. "Just round the next corner, dearie. You can't miss it."

Tommy walked up the street to the corner—and almost bumped into Annike carrying her cloth bag.

"I was coming to find you," she said. "I am sorry about yesterday. I was teasing you." She looked down at the sidewalk. "I do that—I used to do that—to my brother."

Tommy decided to forgive her. "Well, I did call you a spy," he said. "This makes us even. I was going for a bite of fish and chips," Tommy replied, halfway inviting her and halfway still a bit put out by her disparagement of his fighting skills.

"I would love a Cornish pastry," Annike said.

"It's called a pasty," Tommy corrected her. "The fish and chips shop is just up the way," he said, pointing.

"So is the pastry—pasty restaurant," Annike said. She dug into her cloth bag. "I've three shillings and six pence," she said, holding out some coins. "I will buy."

Tommy smiled. "You win. Pasties it is."

"There now," she said. "Much better. We start off again, this time on the right feet." To demonstrate, she took Tommy's arm and set off in a kind of marching step.

The pasties in a tiny shop up the street were really quite good, Tommy thought. And he didn't have to spend his own money. Annike took a last sip of her tea, draining the cup. She wiped her face on her paper napkin. "I know you are on the lookout for spies. I think I may have found some."

Tommy was doubtful. "What do you mean? You saw something?"

Annike shook her head. "No, no. I *heard* something. Last night." She got up from the table. "Come back to my house. You will see." She looked at the clock on the wall. "We have to hurry. It's almost time."

As they walked quickly back to Annike's house, she explained, "I finished the wireless last night, or maybe this morning. I was testing it and listening to frequencies when I heard something unusual."

"What?" Tommy asked, hurrying to keep up with Annike.

"It was a broadcast. Very short. Only a few seconds," she replied. "An hour later, it repeated."

As they entered the shed, Annike pointed proudly to the table. "I finished my wireless." The scattered radio parts from last night were now neatly mounted on a wooden board. A small metal plate held two gauges with black knobs. A pair of tubes were plugged into sockets in the rear. A metal key was wired in the front, and an electric cord connected the wireless to the overhead lightbulb socket.

Annike sat down at the device and flipped a switch. A humming noise came out, and a tube glowed. Tommy stood behind her, trying to understand.

Annike looked over her shoulder, pointing to a wooden box next to the table. "Sit on that. Listen." She glanced down at a watch on her wrist, then slowly turned one of the knobs. Hissing and static faded in and out. Annike leaned forward, listening. Then came a series of short crackling noises. Annike took a pen and a piece of paper and wrote furiously.

"They repeat it three times," she said.

Tommy looked at what she was writing: long lines, short lines, more than he could count. Finally the bursts stopped, and the speaker hissed.

"What is it?" Tommy asked. "It sounds like our wireless at home when Mum is trying to find the BBC."

Annike put down her pencil and turned to Tommy. "You do not know Morse code?" She made her "pfft" noise. "You are a dumb head."

Tommy opened his mouth to object, but Annike put her hand on his arm. "I apologize. You are not a dumb head. But your education has been extremely limited." She put her finger to her lips. "Hush, now. They repeat the message in voice. Listen."

The wireless hissed again, and a voice came over the speaker: "The potatoes are doing well this year." A pause, then: "Emily is getting married next week." The hissing stopped.

She took a paper from the cluttered table, showing it to Tommy. "See? Here are all the transmissions I have heard since this morning."

Written on a sheet of paper were the long and short lines with words beneath them. "Aunt Emma has fed the pigs," Tommy read. "Robert has a history test next week." He looked at Annike, puzzled. "This is nothing!" Then he realized. "It's a code! They're secret messages!"

"Of course they are," Annike said. "Such ordinary phrases could be said in a telephone call or written in a letter. They are short so as to avoid detection. Anyone who heard them might think it was just static. They are sent only at certain hours."

"Can you find out where they're coming from?"

"It cannot be far. Maybe a kilometer or so. My antenna is small. I will need a bigger one for the signal to reach Sweden. To contact my papa." Tears filled Annike's eyes. Almost angrily, she wiped her cheek with her sleeve. "I am sure these are messages to the Nazis from spies here, possibly about the invasion."

Tommy was alarmed. "The invasion is happening soon!"

"Take them to your father. Perhaps the military already knows about this." Annike handed Tommy the paper she'd been writing on and pointed to the door. "Go now."

At the hotel, civilian and military vehicles were parked on both sides of the street. Inside, Tommy squeezed through the crowds of military men and women, civilians who were coming and going on important errands. More guards and sentries than he'd ever seen stood on alert at the hotel entrance and at the door to the large conference room off the lobby. His father was not in their room, and the tall military policeman at the conference room door shooed him away. "Not now, lad."

"But I've got to see my father! He's Lieutenant Commander Collins. I've important information! Spies are sending secret messages on the wireless!" Tommy waved the paper Annike had given him.

"I'm sure, lad, but it'll have to wait," the sentry said, smiling.

Tommy knew he was being humored, but there was nothing he could do about it. He went outside and around the rear of the hotel to try and peek into the conference room, but there were blackout curtains hung over the windows.

Frustrated, Tommy went back inside the hotel and up to the room. He flopped on the bed, which he hadn't made, and scanned the pages. He hoped to find some clue to make sense of the messages. "I think my friend Jules is sick," "Do not forget to bring an extra coat."

Maybe these messages were exactly as they appeared: innocent chatter between friends. After an hour, Tommy decided to go back to find Annike.

He didn't have far to go. When he came downstairs, he saw her at the front desk talking to Mr. Smith.

"Ah, there's your friend," Mr. Smith said.

Annike turned and saw Tommy. She smiled, and for some reason, Tommy felt himself blushing. "Hello, Thomas," she said.

"Call me Tommy."

Annike stepped over to a corner of the lobby. "Did you tell anyone about the messages?"

Tommy shook his head. "I couldn't find anyone. They're all in there," he said, pointing to the closed doors of the conference room.

"Master Collins," Mr. Smith said beckoning to him. Tommy and Annike went over to the desk. "I was just telling your young lady friend that she has a fellow countryman here at the hotel." Mr. Smith rang the bell, and a few seconds later, van Brugge came out from the office in the rear.

"Ya, Mr. Smith?"

"I thought you might like to meet a fellow Hollander," Mr. Smith said.

"Ach, yes indeed," van Brugge said, smiling. He held out his hand to Annike.

"*Goede Middag! Ik ben Hans van Brugge. Wat is je naam, jongedame?*"

"*Mijn naam is Annike Meier. Ik kom uit Amsterdam. Waar kom jij vandaan?*"

Just as Tommy was about to complain, Hans began speaking English. "I am from Amsterdam also. I lived on Kerkstraat, near the Magere Brug." He turned to Tommy. "In English, that means 'thin bridge.'"

"The English call it the Skinny Bridge," Annike said.

"Of course. Skinny." Van Brugge nodded, smiling. "My English is still not too good."

"We lived on Muldergracht, near the gardens," Annike replied. "Papa had a shop—before the Germans came," she said. "We used to go to the sweet shop on Kerkstraat. Do you know it?"

"Ach! Yes. I remember it. Many children came there."

The three of them went to a corner of the busy lobby and sat. "I think—and Annike thinks—there are Nazi spies here in Southampton," Tommy began. "We—owww!" he said as Annike kicked him in the leg. "What did you do that for?"

Annike stood up. "We have to go now. Mrs. Stein will have tea and blueberry scones for us."

Van Brugge stood up, blocking their way. "Spies? If you know of spies, that is very important. I know the military people, the security people here. Tell me, und I will inform them about this."

Tommy realized Annike had a reason for stopping him. He smiled at van Brugge. "We saw a man watching the ships in the harbor. I thought he was spying."

Annike shrugged. "Thomas is always playing at spies. The man was just watching the ships." She stepped around van Brugge. "Come, Thomas. Tea will be getting cold."

As Annike and Tommy started off, van Brugge took Tommy's arm. "Remember, if you see anything out of the ordinary, come and tell me. I will report it. This is a dangerous time."

Tommy pulled his arm free. "I will certainly do so, Mr. Van Brugge." As they left the hotel, Tommy turned back to see van Brugge watching them.

Annike walked quickly up the street, and Tommy hurried to catch up to her.

"Maybe you are a dumb head, Thomas."

"Call me Tommy," he said. "You didn't trust him. Why?"

"I don't like him. His accent was funny. And he didn't know the English for the Magere Brug." She hurried ahead. "Come. It is almost time for another message. And I have a way of finding the source. Maybe."

Annike unlocked the shed door and they went in. She hooked up the battery to her wireless, waited while it warmed up, then turned a knob. Tommy at first heard only the hiss of static. Annike looked at her wristwatch. "Another minute."

Then they heard the voice: "Rain is likely tomorrow, heavy at times over the channel." The message repeated twice.

Tommy realized, "That's a voice. And it's not a weather report."

"You are right. They are warning the enemy of the invasion."

"We must do something," Tommy said.

"Of course," Annike said. "We will find the source."

"How?"

Annike went to the door and beckoned. "Come, Thomas. I will show you."

Annike went around to the side of the shed, where a ladder leaned against it. Annike pointed to the roof. Tommy looked up to see a wooden pole about two feet tall, with sticks attached to it. Wires ran from it into the shed. "It is called a Yagi antenna. It is for finding wireless broadcasts." She turned to go back into the shed. Tommy started to follow her. Annike held up her hand. "I need you to go up the ladder and turn the antenna. I will listen for the signal."

Annike entered the shed. Tommy wasn't all that happy climbing the ladder, which was a bit unsteady on the rain-soaked ground, but he managed. He took hold of the pole.

Annike called: "To the right. Slowly!"

Tommy could hear the faint hiss of static.

"Now to the left. Again slowly," Annike said. After a minute, she called, "Stop! Stop!" Annike came out the door, pointing toward the harbor. "It's that way. We should go."

Tommy was puzzled. "And do what? Look for someone using a radio?"

Annike smiled. "I am not a dumb head." Tommy thought she wanted to add "like you," but didn't.

"I have a battery," Annike said. "We can follow the signal strength." She went back inside the shed. "Help me, Thomas."

"Call me—" Tommy, stopped with a sigh. "Never mind."

Tommy and Annike came out of the shed, Annike carrying her new wireless and gear and Tommy lugging the automobile battery. After they put the equipment into the cart, Annike connected the battery to the wireless and switched it on.

The clouds were gathering that afternoon as Tommy and Annike walked down the hill from the bombed-out St. Michael's church. Tommy wheeled the garden cart over the rough cobblestones while Annike held up a small antenna.

"If these broadcasts must go a long distance, the antenna will be very high," Annike said, thinking aloud.

"On a hill or a building," Tommy finished.

"The signal is strong. I think we are near."

They walked in front of a two-story tenement house with its windows boarded up and a bomb-blasted, shattered side. As they passed the side yard, with bushes around it, a red-haired boy about sixteen years old, and wearing grease-stained blue coveralls, poked his head up.

"What are you two about?" he asked in a strong Irish accent. He walked over and stood in front of them.

"We're exploring," Tommy replied. "Do you live around here?"

"None of your business, English," the boy said with a sneer. "And you'd be wise to explore somewhere else. This is our neighborhood."

Annike stepped forward. "My name is Annike." She held out her hand. "What is your name?"

The boy pushed her hand aside. "Sean, not that it's your business." He looked in the cart and began poking around among the wireless gear. "What's all this, then?"

Annike leapt at Sean and pushed him away. "Leave that be!"

Sean shoved Annike, and she fell backwards, overturning the cart and dumping its contents. A glass tube shattered, and wires came loose. Tommy pushed Sean away.

Sean grabbed Tommy by the shirt front and pulled him close. "Bloody toff! You made a big mistake!"

All-in Fighting, page twenty, Tommy remembered. He took hold of Sean's thumb with both hands and bent it back.

"Ahh! Damn you!" Sean cried out, letting go of Tommy and holding his thumb. Then he swung his good hand and punched Tommy hard in the chest. Tommy fell, hitting his head on the cobblestones.

He'd read in books about people seeing stars, but this was the first time it had happened to him. His vision blurred, then he was looking up at the cloudy sky. He sat up in time to see Annike kick Sean in the knee, a tactic he remembered from their first—or was it the second? —encounter.

Sean bent over, rubbing his leg. "You're just lucky I don't beat up little girls," he said. He limped back up the stairs to the house. "You two had better be gone," he said with a smirk. "My uncle hates the Brits even more than I do."

As he closed the door, Annike yelled after him, "I am Dutch!"

Tommy helped Annike right the cart and put the spilled equipment into it. Annike, angry, held a broken tube. "Look. This was part of my wireless. I do not have another. I've pirated everything useful from Mr. Woolsey's shop." She threw the shattered tube down. "Now we cannot even find that transmitter."

Tommy smiled. "Maybe we can. When I was on the ground looking up, I saw something." He pointed across the street to another bombed building, roofless with just the front and side walls standing, the insides filled with piles of rubble. On the side wall stood the remains of a brick chimney. A black wire extended from the top of the chimney, stretching across and over a narrow alley to a power pole in the backyard of a neighboring house. "That's an antenna, right?"

A broad grin broke over Annike's face. "Yes!" She ran across the street, picking her way carefully over the piled brick and splintered wood siding. She stared down at the remains of the house floor, then she ran back to Tommy. "I think there is an intact basement under all that. There are two wires twisted together. One is likely the antenna, and the other draws power from the pole for the wireless." She patted Tommy on the cheek. "I think you are definitely not a dumb head."

Tommy looked around, then smiled and pointed down the street. "I'll put the cart behind that pile of stone. We need to alert the police."

Tommy and Annike hurried down the hill to the police station. It was almost as busy as the rest of town. Bobbies, many wearing military helmets, hurried in and out the door of the ancient stone building. Inside, a white-haired constable was dealing with a half-dozen local folks, all talking at once.

"Upper Bar road is closed."

"Can you get the gas turned again?"

"A lorry's blocking the street in front of my house."

Annike and Tommy stood at the rear of the crowd for ten minutes, trying to stop other people from cutting in front of them.

Finally, Annike had had enough. She pushed her way to the front and climbed atop the constable's desk. "There's a hidden wireless on Bayswater Road transmitting coded messages."

"Get off my desk, young lady!"

Tommy shoved his way to the front of the crowd. "You have to listen. There are Nazi spies!"

A man in the crowd chuckled. "Nazis, indeed!"

Annike jumped off the constable's desk. "We can show you—"

The constable interrupted her, calling out, "Sergeant, would you see to these youngsters?"

A younger man with a bushy moustache, with three stripes on his blue jacket, came over. "What's all this, then?" He led Tommy and Annike to a paper- and file-covered desk at the rear of the stationhouse.

"We have found a hidden radio sending coded messages," Annike said.

"Nazi spies, maybe saboteurs," Tommy chimed in.

"Well, well. You two have uncovered a nest of spies, eh? Good work. You'd better report this to the military authorities."

"I tried. They're all occupied with planing," Tommy said. He took the now wrinkled paper with the messages from his pocket and showed them to the sergeant. "Look here. These are the messages."

The sergeant scanned the paper. "Flowers are blooming later this year. James found a bird's nest in the old oak tree." He stroked his moustache. "These could be coded messages." He waved his hand, indicating the constables hurrying back and forth. "As you can see, we're quite busy ourselves. But I will notify the military personally." He took a pen from the desk and a notebook. "What's the location?"

Annike described the ruined house. The sergeant again nodded. "Thank you. It's alert young people like yourselves that help us keep our country safe." He picked up a telephone. "We'll get on this right away."

The sergeant watched Annike and Tommy as they left the station house. He put down the phone and chuckled. "Nazis, secret codes, hidden radios."

The constable at the front desk turned around, nodding. "Those fishermen caught one spy, and now everyone's finding Germans in their gardens!"

The sergeant crumpled the paper he'd been writing on and the messages into a ball, aimed and tossed it into a waste bin.

Tommy helped Annike put the broken bits of her wireless back on the desk in the shed. She was sad. "I do not know how I can put this together in time to talk to Papa."

Tommy smiled. "I know someone who might help. Lieutenant Shaffer. He's a wireless operator."

Annike shook her head. "Tomorrow is my day to contact my father!"

Tommy frowned. "We have to try. Let's go find him."

Tommy and Annike hurried down the hill toward the hotel. Tommy stopped at Bugle Street. "It's almost dark," he said. "Let's walk by the house with the antenna. Perhaps the police are there."

Annike smiled. "Not only not a dumb head, but clever—at times."

"And I'm almost never wrong," Tommy said, smiling back at her.

The street was dark. A few workers came out of the rooming houses heading to the dock. As they walked by the bombed-out house, they saw no police vans in evidence.

"That sergeant was just having us on," Tommy said.

"I thought so too," Annike said. She stopped and pointed. "Look. A light."

A thin shaft of light shone between two boards covering a basement window. It was almost invisible from the street. Only someone looking for it would notice. Keeping her torch pointed at the ground, Annike walked over the broken brick and smashed stone towards the house. She bent down and peered inside.

"See anything?" Tommy whispered. He bent down next to her. Nothing could be seen except for a cracked brick wall and a wooden chair.

"Shh." Annike put her finger to her lips.

A faint voice came from inside. An Irish accent. "...at what time?"

Annike and Tommy heard a static-filled hiss. Tommy straightened up and took Annike's arm. "Come on!"

Suddenly Tommy and Annike were seized from behind, hoisted by the scruffs of their necks. A gruff Irish voice growled, "A pair of wee nosy parkers here!" The two were yanked around to see a huge, bearded man scowling at them as he held them in midair like ragdolls.

A voice came from the basement. "What's up, Harry?"

Harry, the giant, threw Tommy and Annike to the ground. Annike started to get up but stopped when Harry reached behind his back and pulled out a pistol that he pointed at them.

"Hey, Harry!"

"Don't get yer knickers in a twist," Harry yelled back. "I'll be down in a second. With a pair of visitors." He motioned with the pistol for Tommy and Annike to get up, then he pointed to the rear of the ruined house. The two walked ahead of him.

A wooden cellar door was set in the ground at the rear, hidden from the street by piles of broken brick and sticks of wood. "Open the door, laddie." Tommy bent down and tugged at the latch. "Put yer back into it," Harry growled.

Tommy managed to pull the door open, then let it fall to the side, clattering atop the rubble. Light washed out, showing a cement stairway leading down. Harry waved his pistol. "Down ye go." Tommy and Annike went down the stairs, and Harry pulled the door shut as he followed behind.

A single gas lantern illuminated the basement, showing a pile of lumber, a pair of chairs tucked under a desk, a workbench with a tattered leather suitcase containing a wireless and microphone in it, and a stack of papers. A thin, balding man looked up nervously. "What's this?" he asked in a quavering voice. "No one's supposed to be here."

"I found 'em poking about outside," Harry said. He pointed with the pistol to the single boarded-up window. "You was supposed to make sure we were light tight, Gavin."

Gavin stood up and hurried to the window, pushing on the nailed-up wood. "I did!" he whined. "One of these boards must have slipped."

Harry shrugged. "No matter. We'll be gone soon."

Gavin nodded his head towards Tommy and Annike, who were huddled together in a corner. "What do we do with them?" He looked at Harry, then looked away. "You can't—"

Harry grinned. "Do 'em in? Nah, although I did think on it. Don't need killing kids on my conscience." He pointed to some rope hanging on a nail on the wall. "Tie 'em up."

Gavin pulled the rope off the nail and went over to Tommy and Annike. "Hands behind you." Both frightened, they did as they were told.

He finished tying their arms behind their backs then gestured. "Sit on the floor. Back to back." Gavin tied the two together. "Now what? Just leave 'em here by themselves?"

Harry shook his head. "They might make some mischief. Get yer nephew to keep an eye on 'em whilst we finish our business."

Gavin shook his head. "Sean's got nothing to do with this."

Harry shrugged. "It don't matter. We'll finish the work and be gone soon. Anyways, what's he to do? He's stuck with us." He tucked the pistol in his belt, reached under the bench and pulled out a brown canvas bag that he hoisted over his shoulder. He looked at his watch. "You and Sean pack yer kits. Our friend will join us here afterwards. He sends the message, whatever he's got, and Bob's your uncle. We're off, clean as a whistle." Harry went up the stairs and out, the door slamming behind him.

Gavin turned off the wireless and got up, taking a last look at Tommy and Annike. Then he went up the cellar stairs.

Tommy was more afraid than he had ever been: afraid for himself and afraid for Annike. "I'm sorry," he began, but Annike interrupted him.

"No, I am sorry," she said, turning her head as far as she could to see him out of the corner of her eye. "I was too eager to prove myself right. We could have told the police."

"We tried that," Tommy said. "They just dismissed us." He tried to turn his head to look at her. "You're very brave. Although you're also a dumb head."

Annike couldn't help smiling a bit. "I am."

The cellar door opened, and they saw feet coming down the stairs. It was Sean. He stared at them.

"You two!" He came over and stood above them. "I warned you to stay away."

"You betray your country. For what?" Annike said.

"Ireland is my country," Sean said angrily. "The bleedin' Brits have ground us down forever. The damned Black and Tans have killed our people."

"And you think that sabotaging the invasion, helping the Nazis, will help Ireland?" Annike asked.

Sean grew red in the face. He paced the floor angrily. "We're not sabotagin' nuthin'," he said. "I came with my uncle and Harry because there's work. And I hate the bloody Germans. I seen what they done."

"He doesn't know," Tommy whispered to Annike. But in the tiny room, it might as well have been a shout.

"I don't know what?" Sean asked, still pacing. "What I know is, my uncle told me to keep an eye on two thieves they'd caught tryin' to steal the wireless. That's you two. They've gone to get the coppers."

"Why do you have the wireless?" Tommy asked. "And why are you hiding it in a basement?"

Sean looked confused. "Well, Uncle Gavin and Harry use it to talk to home. The phone service is down sometimes. And I talked to me mum Thursday last. Told her I'm doin' all right." His face softened. "I miss her and my da. But the pay is good."

"Untie us, please," Annike said. "These ropes hurt so much." She sniffled.

Sean shook his head. "I can't. Harry'll have a fit."

"We promise not to try and escape," Tommy said. "Besides, you could stop us."

Sean paced some more, thinking. Finally he said, "All right. But if you try anything, I'll do you like I did before." He untied their ropes and pointed to a corner of the basement. "Sit there. If you twitch, I'll beat you 'til you can't stand up."

Tommy and Annike rubbed their arms, reddened from the ropes. They went to the corner and sat on the floor.

Annike pointed to the wireless. "Have you sent coded messages?"

Sean scoffed. "Coded messages? To me mum? I come down here once or twice a week, when I'm not working, and we have a chat is all."

"Take a look at those papers," Tommy said. "Those are messages your uncle and Harry are sending. When you aren't here."

With his eye on them, Sean picked up the pile of papers and read them. He frowned, running his hands through his mop of red hair. "I never seen these before." He read some more. "We don't have an Aunt Emma. This don't make no sense."

"Turn the wireless on," Tommy said. "Maybe you'll hear something."

Sean sat down, staring at the box with its dial and meters. "I never worked this. Gavin just tunes it up, and I talk to Mum."

Annike got up and crossed to the desk. Sean turned as if to grab her. "Move," she said. "I know how to do this." Sean got up, and she sat in the chair. She flipped a switch, and the meters glowed. "Wait until it gets warm." She stared at the dial. "Hmmm, one-seventy-three point six. Maybe someone is still listening on the other end."

Annike pushed a button on the microphone, leaned forward and spoke into it. "*Hallo. Das ist ein Notfall.*"

All they heard was static. Annike tried again. "*Hallo. Das ist ein Notfall.*"

Then a man's voice said, "*Wer ist das?*" More static and hissing, then, "*Wer ist das?*"

Annike flipped the power switch, and the meters went dark. She looked up at Sean, who was standing over her. "Does your mum speak like a man? In German?"

Tommy watched a boy fight with himself, it seemed. Then Sean began to crumble. He was seeing everyone he trusted, everyone he believed in, had been hiding behind masks. He opened his mouth to say, "That's not…I never heard…" He stopped, turned away, pacing back and forth. Then he pointed at Annike. "You changed something!"

"You were watching me. I changed nothing."

Sean bowed his head, shaking it side to side. Almost to himself he muttered, "It's the damned IRA."

Tommy saw Annike's questioning look. "The Irish Republican Army. They want freedom from British rule of Ireland. There was something on the news about it. Some are Nazi sympathizers," Tommy explained.

Sean got up, went to a pile of wood scraps in a corner, picked up a stout piece, and came towards Tommy and Annike. They backed up, frightened, but Sean stepped past them and raised the wood, ready to smash the wireless. "I don't care if he's my uncle! I don't care if Harry kills me!"

Annike quickly blocked Sean. "No. I need that."

Sean dropped the wood and slumped into the chair. He looked up. "Now what do I do?"

"Do you know where they were going?" Tommy asked. "We could alert the military."

Sean shook his head. "There's no time. Gavin told me we're leaving tonight at midnight." He looked at his watch. "That's two hours from now." He thought for a moment. "Harry's got some kind of delivery van."

"Whatever it is they are planning, it's going to happen soon. We must inform someone," Annike said.

Tommy nodded then turned to the still-distraught teenager. "You aren't a part of this. You can go to the police, tell them what you know."

Annike bent over Sean, still slumped in the chair. "Or you could just pack your kit and go back home." She knelt in front of him. "I know what it is like to lose your family. Even though your uncle is not gone, he is lost to you. But you must live your life."

Sean looked at her then stood up. "I'll figure it out." The three of them stood there for a minute, a sad tableau. "I reckon I'll go." He nodded to Annike, managing a tiny smile. "Thanks." Sean went up the stairs and disappeared into the dark.

Annike unplugged the wireless from the wires. She took a coil of wire, tucked it into the suitcase, and closed it, snapping the latches. She lifted it off the desk. "Ugh! This is heavy." She held it out to Tommy. "Here."

Tommy, ever confident, took hold of the handle— and dropped the bag to the floor.

"It is a bit heavy, I'd say."

"Do not damage it!"

"You could help instead of giving orders," Tommy said. Annike took one end and Tommy the other, and they went up the stairs. At the top, in the darkened back yard, Tommy motioned for Annike to set the case down. He went back into the cellar and switched off the light.

The two of them, straining and sore, managed to carry the heavy case through the pitch-dark streets for a half-mile.

"This'll take all night," Tommy said, putting his end down on the ground. "We have to tell the authorities."

Annike grabbed the handle and struggled to lift it. "Fine. You go."

Tommy took the case from Annike and stepped away from her. She tried to get it, but he held on. "No! We both go. You go tell the military about the Nazi wireless signal. People are in danger now from those IRA traitors."

Annike sat down on the street, her head in her hands. "It's the only chance I have. *Om mijn vader te vinden.*"

Tommy understood *"mijn vader."* He sat down next to Annike and put his hand on her shoulder. She pulled away.

"I know you need to talk to your father. I don't know what it's like, what you've been through," he said. "But I do know we have to try and stop those men." He looked around, then took Annike's shoulder again. Tommy pointed to a car sitting on its axles in a drive next to a bomb-damaged house. "We'll hide the wireless in the boot of that car. Come back for it as soon as we can. We'll be back before daylight. No one will see it." He stood up and held out his hand to Annike. "I'll make sure that you'll be able to send a message to your family. On your birthday."

Annike took Tommy's hand and stood up. They faced each other for a moment, then she hugged him. Tommy did not know what to do except hug her back.

Together they carried the suitcase to the car. Tommy opened the boot, and they put the wireless in.

"We've got to tell my dad," Tommy said, grabbing Annike's arm and hurrying down the street. "He'll be at the hotel."

CHAPTER

Monday, 5 June 1944

"We'd better hurry," Tommy said as they ran down the street.

"We know where they are," Annike said.

"But they won't be there for long," Tommy replied.

As they arrived at Canute Road, with the South West Hotel just ahead, an explosion shook the ground, staggering Tommy and Annike.

"A bombing raid!" Tommy exclaimed. He looked up to see a pillar of smoke coming from behind the hotel.

Tommy ran faster, tugging Annike's hand. "Run. There's a shelter at the hotel."

Searchlights came on. They swept the skies, lighting up the barrage balloons, giant blimp-like things floating above. A group of soldiers leapt into the sandbagged gun battery at the bottom of the street and quickly mounted their gun. They cranked the wheel to raise the twin barrels then swiveled it around to look up into the dark.

The street was crowded with people heading for the nearest shelter. ARP men, in helmets and wearing gas masks, herded stragglers along. "Hey, you two!" one of them called out. "The shelter's the other way!"

Tommy and Annike ignored him and hurried on. They reached the front door of the darkened hotel, where a British MP was ushering people inside. An air raid siren sounded nearby, and people hurried through the doors. In the lobby, a throng of people came downstairs from the upper floors and walked swiftly to the narrow stairs leading to the basement.

Tommy's father was waiting in the lobby, visibly relieved as Tommy came in.

"Where in the hell—" He stopped himself. "We'll talk later. Come on." He saw Annike for the first time. "Who's this?"

"My name is Annike Meier," she said, holding out her hand, a calm center in the midst of the chaos.

Lawrence shook it. "Pleased to meet you," he said. "We've got to get to the basement shelter." He moved to the stairs, beckoning to Tommy and Annike to follow.

As they followed Tommy's father, another explosion, even closer, tossed Tommy to the floor. Tommy got up, his ears ringing. The lobby filled with smoke and dust.

Near the basement entry door, his father reached down to help a woman who'd fallen. Annike, at the top of the stairs, was holding onto the banister and coughing.

"Come on!" Tommy shouted, hearing his own voice as if from far away. Annike shook her head.

What's she on about? Tommy wondered. He ran back up the stairs.

Annike spoke, but he couldn't hear her. He pointed to his ears and shook his head. She shouted. "Those explosions. They were not aerial bombs."

"How do you know?" Tommy yelled at her.

"Amsterdam was bombed many times when the Germans invaded our country," Annike yelled back. "We could hear the planes overhead. We could hear the bombs falling, screaming like demons. I know. I know." Outside, the siren stopped. "See? No planes. No air raid." She looked away for a moment then pointed. Annike hurried to the door, still coughing, and looked out.

Tommy heard a groan from behind the front desk. "Wait!" he yelled. "Someone's hurt!" They ran over. Mr. Smith lay on the floor, his eyes closed, a bleeding gash on his head. "Annike!" Tommy called. "Come here!"

She bent down over Mr. Smith to examine his injury. "It is a surface wound only," she said. She riffled through the shelves under the desk and pulled out a torch and a wooden box with a red cross on it. Inside were bandages, a bottle of antiseptic, and gauze. She handed Tommy the torch. "Hold this," she said. Tommy shined the torch on Mr. Smith's forehead. Annike took a square of gauze and put it on the bloody cut, pressing the gauze to Mr. Smith's head.

Mr. Smith moaned and opened his eyes. He coughed. "Is...safe...?"

"Uh, is what safe?" Tommy asked.

Mr. Smith groaned again and shook his head feebly. "No...no. The safe. The safe." He coughed. "It...was van Brugge."

Annike's eyes widened. She stood up, peering through the smoke. She pulled Tommy to his feet.

Across the smoky lobby, they saw van Brugge carrying a briefcase. He opened the door to the operations center and looked around. Then he ran out the front entry.

Annike took the torch Tommy held, then ran across the lobby, the beam cutting a path through the dark. Tommy couldn't see her. Then he heard her: "Tommy, come here."

Mr. Smith struggled to sit. He put his hand over the wound on his head. "I'm all right. Go." He stood up and staggered to an upholstered chair, where he sat down hard. He still held the gauze to his head.

Tommy got up and ran towards Annike's voice, bumping into lobby furniture along the way. Annike was standing by the door of the dark meeting room. The door was open, and Annike stared inside. She shined the light into a corner of the room. The safe that Tommy had seen when he toured the room yesterday was blown open, the door hanging by a single hinge. Papers and files were scattered on the floor in front of it.

"This was the second explosion," Annike said.

"Oh no!" Tommy said. "Operation Overlord…the invasion plans." He looked around as if expecting to see the guilty party. "The Dutchman. Van Brugge!"

"He's not Dutch. He's a German. A Nazi," Annike said. Tommy and Annike hurried to the front door and ran outside. They peered up and down the street. Up Canute Road, it was dark. Tommy and Annike ran around the corner.

Across Terminus Road, in Queen's Park, they saw a small smoking crater. Annike peered at it. "That wasn't an aerial bomb. It would have blown out the hotel windows."

"It was a diversion to get everyone into the shelter," Tommy said.

"Was I correct about van Brugge?" Annike asked.

"You may not say, 'I told you so,'" Tommy replied. "He's going to tell the Nazis about the invasion."

Annike nodded. "But we have hidden their radio." She hurried toward the hotel lobby, adding, "And I told you so."

"Sean said they have a van," Tommy said. "They'll get away. We don't know where they're going."

Annike started up the steps into the hotel. "We have slowed them down, but we have to stop them. We have to warn the military."

Tommy thought for a minute. "There's no need. They'll see the safe. The documents are missing. Mr. Smith will tell them about van Brugge. We have to find out where they're going."

Annike came back down the steps. "That Nazi has a head start. They could be gone already," she said.

Tommy took the torch from Annike's hand. "You tell my father," he said. "I've got to do something." He went out the front door.

At the front of the hotel, an ARP warden walked up the street, calling out, "All clear. All clear." At the end of Canute Road, the ack-ack gun crew was busy unloading the weapon. Tommy watched for a minute, then strolled down the street to join the few other people who had come out of their shelters. In the distance, a searchlight illuminated a barrage balloon that was slowly deflating and sinking to the ground.

Tommy crouched low and crossed the street to the sandbagged gun emplacement. Two bicycles, no doubt belonging to the gun crew, were leaning against the sandbags. Staying out of sight, Tommy took hold of one bicycle's handlebars and pushed it round the corner.

He was looking over his shoulder at the crew when he bumped into a woman coming out of a door. "Watch where you're going, young man."

The crewmen in the emplacement turned to look. "That's my bicycle! Come back!"

Tommy pushed past the startled woman and hopped on the bicycle, pedaling furiously. The seat was too high, so he stood on the pedals as he sped up the street. "It's an emergency! I'll bring it back!" he yelled over his shoulder. "I promise!"

Van Brugge had a head start, but Tommy thought he could get there faster. It wasn't as easy as that. Going up the hill from the hotel to the hideout, he had to pedal furiously. His pantleg got caught in the chain, and he had to stop and free it. As he came round the corner onto Bugle Street, he almost collided with a military jeep speeding down the hill, its lights out.

The street was pitch dark. Tommy leaned the bicycle against a tree a half-block away. Moving behind bushes and in the shadows of darkened houses, he made his way to the bombed-out tenement, where he hid behind a pile of bricks and broken lumber. A red Austin van was parked in front of the bombed house. *That must be the van,* Tommy thought. He knew what he had to do. Just then, he heard voices coming from the street behind him. He scrambled behind a pile of rubble.

Harry and Gavin walked by on their way to the boarding house.

"Get yer stuff. We're leaving." Harry said.

"Of course. Van Brugge ought to be here pretty soon. You think he got what he was looking for?" Gavin replied.

"Our Nazi friend seems pretty capable." Harry laughed. "You heard those explosions?"

The two men crossed the rubble-strewn street and went into the boarding house. As soon as they went inside, Tommy hurried over to the Austin van. He knew what he had to do. He had to stop the saboteurs—or at least slow them down.

Tommy examined the front, looking for a way to open the bonnet. The van was nothing like his father's Humber, which had a chrome bonnet latch by the front fender. He tried the driver's door, but it was locked. Frustrated, Tommy kicked at the tire. He had to work quickly before Gavin and Harry returned.

He grabbed the bonnet ornament, trying to lift the bonnet—and the ornament turned! He twisted it, and the bonnet popped up! It was heavy, but he managed to raise it high enough to see inside. In the rear of the engine compartment, he saw the black cylinder with a wire on top. The coil. Tommy stood on the bumper and leaned forward into the engine compartment to reach it. He had to let go of the bonnet, and it came down on his back. It hurt. He pulled on the wire. One end came loose from the coil, the other end from what Tommy remembered was the distributor. Holding the wire, Tommy strained to lift the bonnet. He slid out from under, scraping his back on the bonnet's metal edge.

Tommy's foot slipped off the bumper, and he lost his hold on the bonnet. It came down with a metal crash. Just then, he heard the door of the boarding house open. He ducked behind the front of the van and peered around it. Harry and Gavin, both carrying luggage, were coming down the steps,

"What was that?" Harry asked, shining his torch into the drive where the van was parked.

"I didn't hear anything," Gavin replied as they crossed the street.

Stuffing the coil wire in his pocket, Tommy ducked low and scrambled to hide behind a car parked in the neighboring drive.

Harry waved the torch beam, looking around. "A cat or something," Harry said.

Tommy turned to see a torchlight down the street held by someone on foot. Harry on one side, the approaching stranger on the other! Fortunately, Harry and Gavin walked back down the drive to see who was coming. Tommy quickly hid behind a bush, dropping to his stomach.

The man passed by Tommy's hiding place. It was van Brugge, carrying the briefcase and walking quickly. And no longer limping. *Part of his disguise,* Tommy thought.

Harry called out, "Look who finally got here."

"Never mind that," van Brugge said. "We must hurry. They will be looking for us."

"Looking for you, maybe," Harry said with a snort.

Gavin unlocked the van and put the luggage in the rear. He followed van Brugge and Harry to the basement. After a minute, Harry yelled, "Where's the damn wireless? Where's Sean?"

Another voice, probably Gavin's, said something Tommy couldn't hear.

Another voice spoke. "Not to mind." It was van Brugge. "We will go to the other location. I can radio from there. The invasion fleet is just leaving the harbor. They will be four or five hours crossing the channel."

"We'd better go," Gavin said. "I'll make a last look-see for Sean." Tommy ducked down as Gavin hurried across the street. After a minute, he hurried back. "His motorbike is gone. He took his kit. Maybe he—"

"If you want him alive, you'd better hope he's gone." Harry growled. "So help me God, nephew or not, I'll kill him!"

"We have to leave," van Brugge said. "He might go to the authorities."

"Sean would never do that!" Gavin said.

"We cannot take that chance. We leave. Now."

Harry unlocked the van door and got in, van Brugge and Gavin following.

Rrr-rrr-rrr—the van motor cranked over. Harry tried again. Rrr-rrr-rrr. And again and again. Harry got out. "Blasted thing won't start." He opened the bonnet and shone his torch into the motor compartment. "Bloody hell!"

Gavin got out and looked. "The coil wire's gone!"

Harry said, "Somebody's pirated it. Sean."

"Stop blaming him for everything!" Gavin almost shouted.

"We can get another. We must hurry," van Brugge said.

"We'll steal one." Harry looked around, shining his torch up the dark street.

Tommy silently backed away, keeping the car between him and the others. Then he turned and ran down the street. He got on the bicycle and pedaled as fast as he could, heading for the hotel. He leaned the bicycle against the wall of a building near the ack-ack installation and ran up Canute Road to the South West Hotel.

The sentry at the front door stopped Tommy from going in. "What's your hurry, lad?" he said.

"I need to speak to someone." Tommy replied, breathless from his ride. "My father is Lieutenant Commander Collins. Nazi spies have stolen secrets vital to the war effort. They're going to inform the Germans of the invasion."

The sentry nodded. "We know all about it. We're looking for them now."

"I know where they are!" Tommy exclaimed. "I need to tell my father. He's just inside."

"Wait here, lad. Most everyone's left. I'll find someone. We'll sort this out." The sentry went inside. Tommy sat on the steps, fidgeting.

Moments passed. No one came out. Another minute. Tommy got up to go into the hotel when he heard the roar of an engine.

A motorcycle pulled up with Sean driving and Annike, her hair a tangle, riding in the rear.

"There you are! We've been looking everywhere!" she said, hopping off as Sean came to a stop.

"I'm going to tell my father—"

"Never mind that," Annike interrupted. "I found Sean, and we went back to get the wireless." She patted a canvas bag on the rear of the motorcycle with the brown suitcase sticking out.

"They've gone," Sean said. He put down the kickstand and got off the bike.

"Then it's more important than ever that we let the military know," Tommy said. "They're already looking for them."

"Pfft." Annike made her noise. "They don't even know where to start. By the time they find them—if they find them—that Nazi will already have contacted the Nazis."

"I know where they're going," Sean said.

"If we hurry, I can stop their broadcast with this," Annike said, patting the bag with the wireless again.

"We should go now!" Sean said. He got on the motorcycle and kicked the starter. The engine started with a quiet rumble. Tommy swung his leg over the pillion seat, but Annike pulled him off. "I ride there," she said. "You sit on this thing." She pointed to the metal rack over the rear wheel. She climbed on, putting her arms around Sean. Tommy got on the rear, the most uncomfortable seat he'd ever sat on. The metal cut into his legs, and his feet dangled close to the ground. Sean put the bike in gear, and they took off. Tommy almost fell off backward, grabbing Annike's waist. They wound their way around Southampton's dark streets and up the hill to the Itchen bridge.

"Where are we going?" Tommy yelled.

"Sean knows," Annike yelled back. She smiled, enjoying the ride. Tommy was not. Sean seemed to hit every bump in the road. Tommy clung tightly to Annike, thinking the next pothole would toss him off.

Sean drove as if he could see the road, although the only illumination came from the thin gap in the black paint covering the headlamp. Annike turned her head. Tommy could see her smiling, the wind blowing through her hair.

After a bumpy fifteen minutes, Sean slowed down and guided the motorbike off the road.

"Harry and my uncle found an abandoned pub just ahead. They'll likely already be there. We might be too late."

Tommy climbed off, rubbing the sore spots on his legs. He lifted the wireless case out of the saddlebag. "We have to try."

Sean turned off the motor. "They'll hear the bike. Help me push it." Tommy and Annike pushed from the rear, and Sean guided it. Together they rolled the machine to a shuttered petrol station and parked it behind a small lorry.

Sean pointed into the dark. "The pub is next door," he said quietly.

Annike took out the suitcase, squatted next to it on the ground, and opened it. "Maybe I can still block their transmission," she whispered. She connected the battery and turned on the wireless. Two lights on the front lit up.

Tommy walked past the parked lorry and through the darkened street to the pub. He crouched low and crept up to the front window. The inside was dim, lit only by two lanterns, Van Brugge was hooking up a battery to a wireless atop the mahogany bar, whilst Harry paced the floor.

Gavin sat at the bar, a glass in his hand. "The boat will be at Burnham in two hours. If we're not there, they'll leave."

"Shut up, Gavin," Harry snarled. "You've been whingeing non-stop. Do something."

"The radio is ready," van Brugge said, holding out a loop of wire to Gavin. "String this up outside. As high as you can."

Tommy scrambled back quickly to hide behind the lorry at the petrol station. Gavin came out the door and draped the antenna wire on some bushes. Then he tossed a loop over a tree by the side of the building.

Tommy glanced over his shoulder. He saw Annike and Sean huddled over the wireless by the petrol pumps.

"First we try the frequency they were using before," Annike whispered.

Tommy watched as Gavin looked around then went back into the pub. Tommy whispered to Annike and Sean, "They're just about to send their message."

Annike flipped a switch on the wireless. The tubes glowed, and the dials lit up. "I do not know if I can block their signal. But I can alert our people." She took out the Morse code key and tapped quickly. "I will tell them where we are." She looked at Sean. "Where are we?"

"Southampton Road, Alderbury," Sean said.

Annike clicked on the Morse key. After a minute, the dials grew dim. The tubes went out. "The battery!" She wiggled the wires, then disconnected and reconnected them to the battery, with no result.

Sean squatted over the wireless. "We can hook this up to the motorbike battery," he said. "Half a mo."

Sean pulled a side panel off the motorbike to expose the battery. He wrapped the bare ends of the wire around the battery terminals. The wireless lit up. Annike gave him a hug, and Tommy experienced that uncomfortable feeling again.

Annike turned the dial. Static and hissing. Then: "*Beachtung. Das ist der Holländer.*" A hissing came from the speakers on the wireless. "*Beachtung…beachtung.*"

Annike looked up. "That's them!"

"*Gottverdammt!*" That last came through the door of the pub. "The signal is weak. Check the antenna!" Harry come out the door, gun in one hand, torch in the other. He checked the antenna by pulling on it, then he looked up at the trees.

Tommy, hiding behind the parked lorry, backed away. Annike and Sean were focused on the wireless. There was a loud crackle of static. Harry looked around the dirt yard, then began walking toward the petrol station and the parked lorry. "So…Where are you?"

Tommy crouched down, pointing to the wireless. "Hide that!" he whispered.

Harry was coming closer, sweeping his torch from side to side. Annike shut the case, and Sean quickly slid it under the motorcycle. He stood up and grabbed Annike and Tommy's arms and yanked them to their feet.

"Don't worry," he whispered to them. Then he called out, "Hey, Harry. Look who I found."

Harry came around the parked lorry and shone his torch at them. "Well, well."

Harry shined the torchlight in Sean's face. "*Is fealltóir tú. You are a traitor.*"

Holding Tommy and Annike's arms, Sean walked towards Harry, who pointed his pistol at him. "You stole the wireless. You let those brats go."

Sean took another step forward, pulling Annike and Tommy. He still blocked Harry's view of the motorcycle. "No. They were poking about at the hideout. I brought them here." He shrugged, smiling slightly. "Maybe they poached the radio."

The pub door opened, and van Brugge came out with Gavin behind him. "What's going on?"

Harry waved his pistol at Sean, Tommy, and Annike. "We have visitors."

Gavin looked relieved. "We were worried about you, Sean."

Harry grunted.

Van Brugge waved a pistol. "No more noise. Get them inside." Harry and van Brugge watched as Tommy, Annike, and Sean marched into the pub.

Harry waved his pistol at Gavin. "Your nephew is a traitor. Maybe you are too."

Van Brugge took hold of Harry's pistol arm and pushed it down. "We deal with them later. I need to send this information now."

They entered the pub. Van Brugge pointed with his pistol to a small table in the corner of the pub. "Sit." Sean, Tommy, and Annike sat.

Harry stood over Sean. "You almost fouled us up good, Sean." He swung his pistol and hit Sean on the jaw.

"Ahh!" Sean yelled and fell off his chair. Harry picked him up by his shirt collar and threw him back into the chair, where he slumped down. Harry hit him again. Blood flew out of Sean's mouth.

Gavin stepped between Harry and Sean. "That's enough," he said.

"It's enough when I say so," Harry snarled. "He almost botched our job. Along with his friends." He smiled at Tommy and Annike. It was not a nice smile.

"What do we do with them?" Gavin asked. He looked at Sean.

Van Brugge was at the wireless, tuning it and listening through the static. He turned his head. "When we are finished here, we take them out into the woods and kill them. Maybe not your nephew."

Gavin looked as if he wanted to say something, but Harry grabbed his arm and squeezed it hard.

Van Brugge switched on the microphone and spoke. "*Beachtung. Das ist der Holländer.*" Static came from the speaker. Van Brugge twisted the knob. "*Beachtung. Das ist der Holländer.*"

After a few seconds, a static-filled voice came back. "*Was ist dein Code?*"

Annike whispered, "That's the Nazis. They're asking for a code." She looked away. "We didn't stop them."

Tommy and Annike looked at one another, then at Sean slumped in a booth. He looked over at them. "I'm sorry."

"This was not your fault," Annike said.

"Quiet!" van Brugge said. He spoke into the microphone again. "*Code ist acht sieben vier.*" Static came from the speaker.

"*Bereithalten.*" Another moment, then, "*Fortfahren.*" Another moment, then, "*Fahre fort mit—*" Static broke up the transmission. Van Brugge slammed his hand on the table. "The interference is worse! Go check the antenna."

Gavin went out the pub door. Van Brugge twisted knobs and pulled on wires, but the static hiss continued.

Harry was behind the bar opening a bottle and pouring himself a glass. "Some decent whisky here," he said. "Want some?"

Van Brugge ignored him. He twisted the wireless tuning knob. More static. He looked at Harry. "Go see what is taking Gavin so long."

Harry emptied his glass, then put it down on the bar with a loud clank. "Stop bein' such a bloody maggot. This ain't yer country. Not yet, anyways," he said with a snort. He went out the front door of the pub.

Van Brugge stood up, wiping perspiration from his forehead. He went over to Sean, drawing his pistol. "Now is maybe the time to deal with you."

CHAPTER 9

Tuesday, 6 June 1944

Tommy and Annike exchanged a helpless glance. Van Brugge, pistol in hand, turned as the bell over the pub door jingled.

"Is it fixed?" he asked turning around. His eyes widened as he saw not Gavin or Harry, but two British soldiers, their rifles pointed at him.

Van Brugge's pistol hand twitched. "Don't even think about it," one soldier barked. Van Brugge moved his arm again, and a soldier fired a round, hitting the whisky bottle on the bar, inches away from van Brugge, and shattering it. Broken pieces scattered on the floor.

Van Brugge dropped his pistol to the floor, raising his arms above his head. "You have the advantage."

The first soldier, wearing a white pistol belt and white leggings, pulled van Brugge's arms behind him, clamping handcuffs around his wrists. Then, grabbing him firmly, the soldier took him out the door.

The second soldier came over to Tommy and Annike and helped them stand. "I'm Sergeant Barlow. Are you two all right?" he asked.

"We're fine, sergeant," Tommy said.

Annike grabbed the sergeant's sleeve and pointed to Sean slumped in the chair. "He's been hurt. He needs first aid." Sean tried to sit up but fell back in the chair. "He's not an enemy. He helped us."

Sergeant Barlow turned to Tommy and Annike. "There's no need for you two to be here. Wait outside." He opened the door and called out, "Need a medic in here. Quick."

Tommy and Annike went out the door. A woman in military uniform, wearing a white armband with a red cross on it and carrying a white bag, brushed by them as she went into the bar. Outside, two soldiers guarded van Brugge, Gavin, and Harry, who were seated on the ground, their hands cuffed behind them. A lorry with several soldiers standing beside it was parked at the petrol station.

Annike hurried over to the petrol station, knelt, and pulled the suitcase wireless from its hiding place under Sean's motorcycle. Tommy called to her, "The sergeant said to wait here." She ignored him, turning dials. Static hiss came out. She tapped on the Morse key then waited. Nothing. She tapped again. Annike slipped on the headphones, adjusted the dials, and tried again. Waited. And waited.

After two minutes, she pulled off the headphones, slammed the lid on the wireless, and got to her feet. She walked back to the pub. Tommy saw tears in her eyes. He walked to her, thinking to comfort her, but she turned away from him.

An olive-green Ford saloon pulled into the pub parking lot. Tommy's father got out before it had come to a stop. He ran over to Tommy and hugged him tightly.

"Hi, dad."

"Thank goodness you're not hurt." Lawrence stepped back, putting his hands on his hips. "You put your lives in danger."

"How did you find us?" Tommy asked.

Lawrence nodded to Annike. "Your young friend left a message at the hotel with the frequency of the Nazi wireless. We received part of a Morse message that mentioned Southampton Road." He pointed to the car as Lieutenant Shaffer got out. "The lieutenant tracked the spies' signal, and we got here as soon as we could." Lawrence looked away and wiped his face with his hand. "After the explosion at the hotel, I…I didn't know where you were."

A soldier came out of the pub carrying a grey briefcase. He handed it to Lawrence. "This belongs to you, sir."

Lawrence nodded. "Thank you, sergeant." He opened it and leafed through the contents. "All here."

Lieutenant Shaffer crossed to a corner of the pub where Annike was standing by herself. "Thank you, Annike. If it weren't for you, the Nazis would know all about our invasion plans."

Annike nodded but didn't smile. She looked away. "I am glad. But I still haven't been able to contact my father."

Lieutenant Shaffer took her by the shoulder and turned her to face him. "You won't be able to send from here." He pointed to the pub. "The spies' radio is marginal, and signals here aren't the best." He looked at his watch. "Also, it's after midnight. Pretty late." He smiled. "I've a plan. I spoke about it with Commander Collins. We'll see you in the morning."

Annike snapped out of her funk. "What plan? Where?"

Lieutenant Shaffer patted Annike on her shoulder. "Tomorrow." He walked back to the car, gesturing to one of the soldiers. "Corporal, get that wireless in the petrol station. Put it in the boot of the car."

"Yes, sir." The soldier saluted and hurried across the gravel.

Sean came out of the pub, holding onto the woman's arm. He had a bandage on his lip but managed a wave.

Tommy smiled and waved back. "Thanks, Sean."

Harry, Gavin, and van Brugge were loaded into the back of the lorry. Three armed soldiers climbed in to watch them.

Lawrence beckoned to Tommy and Annike. "Time to go. We've an early morning tomorrow."

Tommy's father got in the front of the saloon, with Lieutenant Shaffer driving and Annike and Tommy in the back.

Annike was fidgeting with her hands and looking out the window as they drove off. "I will hook up the wireless when we get back. I will not sleep until I can talk to my mother and father."

Tommy looked out the window as they went over the Itchen bridge. The harbor was almost empty. The invasion fleet was at sea, heading for France. "The invasion's on," he said, turning to look at Annike. She was snoring quietly.

They drove Annike to her house, then Lieutenant Shaffer dropped off Tommy and his father at the hotel.

In their room, Lawrence pointed to Tommy's bed. "Get some sleep. I have things to handle downstairs."

Tommy went to the window. "I'll watch the harbor for a while," he said. "There's another ship sailing out now." He pulled a chair to the window and sat down.

Five minutes later, Tommy was sound asleep.

CHAPTER

Tuesday, 6 June 1944

Tommy awoke early that morning, finding himself not in the chair but in his bed, with his pajamas on. His father was leaning over him, shaking him gently. "We've got to go."

Tommy went to the loo, washed his face and hands, came out, and put his clothes on. "Are we going home?" Tommy asked realizing that he missed his mum, and even Olivia. "Do we have time for breakfast?"

"Not home. There's a thermos of tea and some blueberry scones in the car," Lawrence said, smiling as if he had a secret. "But don't eat them all."

The sun was poking through clouds as they left the hotel. The family Humber was sitting at the curb. They got in, and Tommy carefully juggled his tea and scone as they went up the dark street, past the now-empty harbor. Lawrence made a left, and Tommy recognized the street. "We're going to Annike's house!"

Lawrence nodded. "You and she have something important to attend to." He pulled the car to a stop.

Annike was waiting on the street under a tree. Without a word, she got in the back seat. Tommy turned, holding out the wrapper of scones and the thermos. "A blueberry scone?" She shook her head, looking out the window at the grey morning. "Tea?" Annike shook her head again. Tommy was sure she was still upset at her failure to contact her father.

As soon as they drove over the bridge, Tommy recognized their destination. "We're going to Southwick House!" he said. He nudged Annike. "Wait 'til you see this! It's where they organized the invasion! A house as big as a castle, a room with giant maps on the walls, soldiers rushing about…" He trailed off. Annike wasn't listening. She gazed out the window.

A few minutes later, Lawrence pulled up in front of the camouflaged stone house.

"Where are we?" Annike asked.

As they got out of the car, Tommy's dad turned and hurried up the stone steps. "You go on in. I've things to do. Lieutenant Shaffer will meet you inside."

Tommy and Annike hurried after him. Tommy opened the door. "Come on. I'll show you where I worked."

As they entered, Annike stopped to stare at the high-ceilinged entry. A dozen soldiers hurried back and forth, up and down the stairs. Tommy took Annike's arm and led her to the communications room and opened the door.

Inside it was even busier than the last time Tommy was there. Every wireless station was occupied, with men and women wearing headphones and talking into microphones or listening and writing rapidly.

Lieutenant Shaffer came up to them. "Good morning, you two."

Annike pointed. "May I use one? Just for a little while?"

The lieutenant shook his head. "Sorry, Annike. All radios are in use. We're a bit busy."

"What about my wireless? Or that one the spies had?" she asked.

"Not available."

Annike nodded, looking away. Lieutenant Shaffer nudged Tommy. "But I've got something to show you. Come with me."

Annike and Tommy followed Lieutenant Shaffer to the rear of the large house. They went out a door leading to a field with some woods beyond.

Annike stopped. "I do not have time for a scenic tour. I must talk to my father."

Lieutenant Shaffer winked at Tommy, putting his finger to his lips. There was a plan afoot.

Tommy took Annike's arm. "Just a bit more, Annike. Then we'll go look for a radio. Come on."

Reluctantly Annike followed Tommy and the lieutenant as they walked up the path to the woods, scuffing her shoes in the gravel.

After a bit, they reached the woods. The path led to a large open space sheltered by trees. A small, olive-green, two-wheeled trailer was parked on the right, a large white star on its side. Two larger, eight-wheeled trailers painted in camouflage sat a few feet away.

Annike looked around briefly then turned to head back down the path. "I have to find a radio."

Lieutenant Shaffer stepped in front of her. "You won't have to go far. Look." He pointed to one of the larger trailers with a tall mast antenna next to it.

Annike looked, then looked again. Her mouth opened, then closed. Before Tommy and Lieutenant Shaffer could react, she ran to the trailer and up the metal steps and pulled on the door. It didn't open. She raised her fist to knock, but just then a young red-haired woman in a British Army uniform opened the door.

She smiled. "You must be Miss Meier. I'm Lieutenant Summersby," she said in an Irish accent. "We've been expecting you." She held the door as Annike stepped inside, Tommy and Lieutenant Shaffer following.

Annike looked at Tommy. "Expecting us?"

The long, narrow room held a dozen desks with teletype machines, phones, and wireless radios. Just beyond was a smaller room, its tables set with cutlery and silverware. Beyond that, an open door revealed stacked military bunks—some beds made, others with sheets and blankets piled on.

Annike gasped, putting her hand over her mouth. "It's…it's so much radio!"

Lieutenant Summersby took Annike's arm and led her to an empty chair at the end of the row of wireless desks. "It took a bit of persuasion, but we managed to keep one free. You'll have a few minutes."

Lieutenant Summersby left as Annike quickly sat down in the chair. She put on the headphones, switched on the power, and turned knobs, watching the meters.

Lieutenant Shaffer sat next to her. "Here, let me…" He reached over, but Annike pushed his hand away.

"I know what to do." She leaned forward, turning the knobs, listening. Static and hissing. She pulled a Morse code key in front of her, plugged it into a port in the wireless, and began tapping.

She waited. Tommy waited. Lieutenant Shaffer waited. Silence. After a minute, Annike tried again. Tap-tap-tap. Pause. Tap-tap-tap.

Silence. Annike tried again. No response. She waited. Silence. She tried again. No response. She grabbed the Morse code key and threw it down. Tears were in her eyes. Annike put her head down. "*Ik weet niet eens of ze nog leven!*" She turned to Lieutenant Shaffer. "I don't even know if they are alive!"

"Are you on the right frequency?" Lieutenant Shaffer asked.

Annike nodded. "We have always the same. And the same day of the year."

Tommy whispered to Lieutenant Shaffer, "It's her birthday."

Annike bent down to pick up the Morse code key, examining it. "I did not break it," she said, putting it back on the desk.

Lieutenant Shaffer reached behind the radio and disconnected two wires. "Wireless traffic is busy this morning, as you might imagine. I'll try something." Holding the wire, he went to the next wireless station, where a severe-looking blond woman in royal Navy uniform was seated. He bent down and whispered something to her. She nodded.

The lieutenant attached the wires he was holding to the rear of her wireless. He came back to Annike. "That'll double the reach of your signal." He adjusted the dials. "Weather and radio traffic are probably making the airwaves crowded. Try again."

Annike pulled the Morse code key to her. She tapped out a series of dots and dashes. She waited.

Tommy waited. More hisses came from the speakers. Annike tapped the key again.

Silence. Annike looked up, a frown on her face. She tapped the code again and again. Nothing but hiss. Annike leaned back in the chair, wiping tears from her eyes.

Lieutenant Shaffer patted her hand. "Keep trying." The noise in the room died down. No one spoke. A man and a woman wandered over to stand behind Annike. Others in the room stopped what they were doing and watched.

Tommy felt impelled to come over and stand behind her. "Try again, Annike. Try again." He put his hand on her shoulder. Giving comfort was not a thing that Tommy did. But he did it. Awkwardly.

Annike keyed in the code again. More hiss came from the speaker. Then, a tapping of code in answer. Lieutenant Shaffer wrote down the code and translated it. "*750...Muldergracht.*"

Annike yelled. "It's our address in Amsterdam! It's Papa!" She quickly tapped a reply, which Lieutenant Shaffer translated. "*Stroopwafel.*" He frowned. "What's that?"

"My favorite biscuit." Annike said. "That tells him I can talk." She took the microphone from Lieutenant Shaffer's hands and switched it on. She spoke into it. "*Papa? Ik ben veilig in Engeland. We moeten Engels spreken.*" She paused, then said, "I'm in England. We should speak English."

A deep, accented voice came from the speaker: "*Ik ben blij…*I am happy to hear your voice, daughter. We are in Malmo, Sweden. We are well."

Tommy heard a cheer. He looked around the room. A half-dozen men and women were standing behind their desks, applauding. Annike clapped her hands. She was crying again, but not sad.

Annike wiped her tears and leaned closer to the microphone. She forgot her English: "*Ik woon in Southampton bij een leuk Joodse familie, Papa.*"

Lieutenant Shaffer got up from his chair, leaned over Tommy's shoulder and whispered: "I think we ought to give Annike some privacy." They left the trailer.

Outside, Tommy looked up as a faint roar grew louder. A flight of planes passed overhead, coming from the northwest. There was a Lancaster bomber, several Spitfire fighters, and other planes.

The lieutenant looked up. "That's flight number ten."

Tommy tried to count them, but he couldn't keep up. There had to be at least a hundred, maybe more.

Annike came out from the communications trailer a few minutes later. Her tears were gone. For almost the first time that Tommy could remember, she had a smile on her face. "My mother, my father, my brother, they are safe." Then she frowned. "But I don't know when I will see them."

Lieutenant Shaffer nodded. "We can hope it'll be soon."

A dark-green car with a four-starred red plaque on the front came up the drive. It came to a stop. A tall, balding man in an American military uniform got out of the driver's seat.

Annike looked puzzled. "Who is that?"

The car's rear door opened, and Tommy's father, Delilah, and Rabbi Stein got out, all smiling. Tommy knew who it was. "General Eisenhower," he said, standing at attention and saluting.

The general smiled. "Good morning." He returned the salute and walked over to Annike and Tommy.

Annike looked at him, started to raise her arm, then stopped. "I am Dutch."

Eisenhower chuckled. "Yes, you are." He held out his hand to Tommy.

Tommy stared at it for a second or two before realizing: the general wanted to shake hands! Tommy shook his hand.

Annike held out her hand. General Eisenhower grasped it in both of his. "I wanted to thank you both personally," he said. "You are both very brave. You took great risks to prevent the enemy from getting our military secrets. I'll see to it that the prime minister and the Dutch government in exile know of your courage."

Tommy blushed. Annike looked down at her feet. Tommy's father, Delilah, and Rabbi Stein gathered around the young heroes and hugged them.

Lieutenant Summersby came out of the small trailer and got into the green sedan, starting it up.

"If you'll excuse me, I've got work to do," General Eisenhower said. "I'm happy your parents are safe, Annike." He got into the saloon's rear seat, and they drove off.

"We'll walk back," Lawrence said as the five of them headed down the gravel path to Southwick House. A flight of planes roared overhead, heading for France and the war.

As they walked, Annike took Tommy's hand. He felt embarrassed and good at the same time.

GLOSSARY

Ack-ack gun – An anti-aircraft weapon

Barrister - A lawyer licensed to defend clients in court

Billets – Living quarters for the military

Biscuit – A cookie

Collegemen – Students at Winchester College

Div – Either a subject of study or a group of students

Form – The English school version of grade levels. First Form is American school sixth grade; Tommy is in second form

Forward – In soccer (British football), a field position closest to the opposing goal

Gevonden! – Dutch for "I found it!"

Going all lobster – Crying

Greensward – Grassy ground

Half-track – a troop transport with tank tracks on the rear and tires on the front

Headmaster – In charge of the school, like a principal in American schools

Home Guard – The armed citizen militia formed by the government in World War II to protect Britain from invasion and sabotage until the regular military forces arrived. Many men and women in this militia were old or retired

Housemaster – In charge of the students in a school boarding house or dormitory

Houses – The dormitories in a boarding school

Huns – A derogatory term for Germans used in World Wars I and II

Kit – Items for a specific purpose, such as work or travel

Leave-out – The school ending time

Lolly – Candy, the term comes from "lollipop"

Lorry – A truck

Lying-in – The practice of staying in bed after childbirth.

Maggot – A grouchy, demanding person

Mucking about – Doing useless things, wasting time

Pasty – A Welsh meat pie

Pitch – The football playing field

Porter – The person responsible for entry to the school, reporting misbehaving students, carrying luggage and overseeing repairs to school property

Prefect – Usually a student in fifth to seventh years who has considerable power; in some cases running the school outside the classroom

RAF – Royal Air Force

Scone – A baked good, like a muffin

Sent down – Expelled or suspended from school

Set-to – A fight

Toady – Someone who always does what the leader wants

Toff – A dandy, an upper-class person

Torch – A flashlight

Whingeing – Whining, complaining

Winkies – Winchester College's name for its unique version of football (American soccer)

Works building – A workshop for school repairs

ADDITIONAL READING

There are a lot of books about World War II in Europe and the Kindertransport. Here are a few:

D-Day: The Invasion of Normandy, 1944, Rick Atkinson

Invasion: The Story of D-Day, Bruce Bliven

The Diary of a Young Girl, Anne Frank

We Had to Be Brave: Escaping the Nazis on the Kindertransport, Deborah Hopkinson

Code Girls: The Untold Story of the American Women Code Breakers of World War II, Liza Mundy

World War II for Kids: A History with 21 Activities, Richard Panchyk

Spies, Code Breakers, and Secret Agents: A World War II Book for Kids, Carole P. Roman

AUTHOR'S NOTE

Dear reader,

Thanks for reading Operation Overlord. If you enjoyed it (even if you didn't!), I'd really appreciate a short review on your favorite online retail bookseller site.

I've got two books you might also be interested in: **She-Wolf**, a young adult novel about a girl whose grandparents are murdered becoming the hunter of the killer; and **Losing Normal**, an award-winning young adult novel about a boy on the autism spectrum who winds up saving us all.

You can download samples from my website: http://www.francismoss.com/books, plus I have included brief samples on the following pages.

I'd love to hear from you. You can email me at francismossbooks@gmail.com, or visit my blog at https://www.francismoss.com to see what I'm up to.

Thanks, and all the best,

ABOUT THE AUTHOR

Francis Moss has written and story-edited hundreds of hours of scripts on many of the top animated shows of the 90s and 00s, including *She-Ra, Princess of Power, Iron Man, Ducktales,* and a four-year stint on *Teenage Mutant Ninja Turtles.* One of his TMNT scripts, "The Fifth Turtle," was the top-rated episode of all the 193 shows in a fan poll on IGN.COM.

He's the co-author of three middle-grade non-fiction books: *Internet For Kids, Make Your Own Web Page,* and *How To Find (Almost) Anything On The Internet,* and sole author of *The Rosenberg Espionage Case.*

EXCERPTS FROM
FRANCIS MOSS' BOOKS

A sample from Francis Moss's
AWARD WINNING novel

LOSING NORMAL

The bell rang at 8:13 AM, and kids began running down the hall to their classes. I started walking to the main hall when Emilio touched my shoulder. I stopped. "Let's wait," he said. A minute and ten seconds later, the hallway emptied and grew quiet. Emilio went ahead and looked around the corner. He waved his hand, which means "come on. "

We walked down the white hallway, staying close to the wall of lockers. We had almost gotten to the door of the Resource Room when Chuck Schwartz, who is my enemy, stepped out of the stairwell. Emilio moved behind me. Chuck Schwartz smiled, but I have seen that smile before. He has a gap between his front teeth. He wore a black T-shirt with no sleeves.

"Hey, Ass-burger!" he said. He walked down the hall toward us, his black boots thumping on the floor. Chuck Schwartz rammed his shoulder into me and smashed me sideways into the lockers. "Watch where you're going, Ass-burger." This was normal.

"I always watch where I'm going," I said, which was stupid. Chuck Schwartz put his hand on my chest and shoved me against the lockers. Emilio backed away, but Chuck Schwartz reached out with his left arm and grabbed him by his shirt. "No, no. You're next. "We stood there for seven seconds. Chuck Schwartz stared at me, and I looked down at the floor, which is what I usually do.

Then I heard a deep voice: "What are you doing?" I looked up to see Mr. Crumley, an older man who volunteers in the library, behind Chuck Schwartz. He has a little white beard and always wears a green tweed jacket and a white shirt buttoned up to his neck.

He put his hand on Chuck Schwartz's shoulder, and Chuck Schwartz let go of us fast. "Just having a conversation, dude."

"Go. Now. Dude," Mr. Crumley said.

Chuck Schwartz headed down the hallway. He turned back and did that thing with his index and middle finger, pointing at his eyes, then at me and Emilio.

"Need a ride home today?" Mr. Crumley asked.

I looked down and shook my head, although I really like Mr. Crumley's red and white 1955 Chevrolet

Bel-Air. Mom had asked him to bring me home a few times when she had to work late at the hospital.

"Thank you, sir," Emilio said.

Mr. Crumley nodded. "Are you all right, Alex?" he asked. I shrugged, which is my default answer. Mr. Crumley turned and walked down the hall. "You're late for class," he said over his shoulder.

A black big-screen monitor hung on the green wall in the Resource Room. This was not normal. Mr. Bates, who usually wore a white short-sleeved shirt and a bow tie, stood behind his desk, next to a blonde woman I'd never seen before. She was wearing a black pant suit and held a tablet computer.

The three other special kids were already there: Bobby turned his head from side to side, going "Woo, woo, woo." Fat Carlos had his head on his desk. The new girl, Sara, who has red hair, freckles, and green eyes, played a game on her phone. She had transferred from another school in the middle of the semester. She looked at me and nodded. "Hey, Rinato," she said.

I stood at the door until Mr. Bates motioned to me to sit down. Emilio went to his regular seat behind me.

Mr. Bates adjusted his glasses and turned to us. "Sara, put your phone away. Everyone, settle down, settle down." We mostly settled down.

Mr. Bates pointed to the monitor. "We've got something special today, class. The Calliope people have come up with a brand-new curriculum, just for us."

He nodded to the blonde woman. She stepped to the front of the class. "Hi. I'm Lucinda Clark and I'm in charge of new technologies at Calliope. Watch this short video; we'll talk about your experiences afterward." She pointed a remote control at the big screen. The man I had just seen on the big screen on Woodbine appeared on this screen, but now he wore long khaki pants and a blue shirt.

"My name is William Locke. You've probably seen me on TV," he chuckled. The blonde and Mr. Bates laughed, but no one else did. "When I was growing up, I had learning problems and behavior problems in school, like some of you. I wish I could have had the program we're about to show you." He smiled. "All right, let's give it a look."

A logo of a yellow sun held in bright blue hands and the word 'Calliope' appeared on the screen. A woman's voice said: "Welcome to Calliope Education! We know that these years of rapid changes in your growing minds and bodies can be challenging and even a little scary at times. This program is designed to help you meet these challenges."

My hands started flapping on my legs. The room disappeared and all I could see were the swarms of fruit flies, spinning like a whirlpool, stretching from the screen, coming at me. My head started to hurt. I closed my eyes and covered my ears with my hands, but I could still see the fruit flies in my head. I tried to push them away.

I heard a crash and opened my eyes. Fat Carlos was sprawled on the floor. Emilio stared at the screen, a little smile on his face. Bobby banged his head on his desk, screaming "Woo! Woo! Woo!" Sara squinted and held her ears. Fat Carlos got up off the floor, then ran out the door, screaming, "Bad! Bad!" Mr. Bates waved his hands in the air, like one of those inflatable things they have in front of stores. My legs started bouncing up and down, my hands flapping. The picture on the screen was a fountain of red and black, filling the room and filling my head, pushing everything else out. My name is Alex. My name is Alex.

I pushed back, there was a loud crash, and everything went away. I opened my eyes and found I was lying on the floor. Sara knelt beside me, holding her head. "Ow! Ow!"

The day before my dad left for Afghanistan, we went to a seafood restaurant on the coast highway. I had a hamburger. When we left the restaurant, the fog had come in, making halos around the lights. I watched out the rear window of our Volvo as we drove away. The lights grew dimmer and dimmer, then disappeared into the gray fog. For three seconds, I remembered something red and black that came from the screen, but then it faded into gray.

I had a headache. I sat up and saw that the monitor was shattered. Pieces of the screen's black glass covered the floor. The blonde woman looked at her tablet, and then she looked at me.

A sample from Francis Moss's
latest MG novel

SHE-WOLF

I woke up in pitch darkness to the sound of an engine and the smell of exhaust. My head hurt where someone had hit me. We went over a bump, and a dim red light flashed. I was in the trunk of a car. My wrists and ankles were tied. I felt something wet and warm running down my head and onto my cheek. Blood. Mine.

I am Deborah Sokolov. I am not dying today.

I twisted around, trying to find something sharp to cut myself free. Another bump, another brake light, and I saw a familiar green blanket stuffed in a corner. I wiggled forward to put my face in it. The blanket smelled of cigars. I was in Grandpa's old Buick.

As I reached behind me to pry up the thin board covering the spare tire, the car came to a stop and I slid forward. A car door, two car doors slammed. The trunk lid opened. I squinted at the flashlight shining in my eyes. Two shadowy figures hovered above me.

"*My ub'yem yeye seychas,*" a gruff voice said in Russian. In Ukrainian, "kill her" is "*vbyy yiyi.*" Different spelling, but it sounds exactly like the Russian.

"*Nyet. My podozhdem,*" a higher-pitched voice replied. Then, in English with a Russian accent: "No. He needs to see her."

The flashlight went out. Two pairs of hands pulled me from the trunk and dropped me onto planks. I was on the boardwalk. The Ferris wheel was still. Behind me was Café Volna, closed and dark. A tiny breeze blew the smell of cooking oil and fish to me. A sliver of the setting moon hung above the water behind Steeplechase Pier, far away down the broad beach.

The two Russians—one tall and skinny, the other short and fat—picked me up and carried me toward the sand. They were wearing black suits, but I'd seen them before in police uniforms. I struggled and fought, trying to get free. The fat one dropped my feet, leaned over, and smacked me with his fist. "Stop it, foolish girl." He hit me where the blood was coming from, and it hurt. He took out a handkerchief and wiped his balding head. "The humidity, Armin. It is *uzhasnyy*, terrible. Even at night."

Armin, the skinny Russian, nodded. "It's the global warming." He bent down, snapped open a switchblade, and cut the ties on my ankles. "She can walk. But," he smiled as he leaned over me and put the knife to my chest, "watch her."

The fat Russian took out a pistol—a silenced Glock 19 with a fifteen-round magazine—and pointed it at me. "Move."

I got to my feet then dropped to my knees, groaning loudly. "My head. It hurts."

"Of course it hurts. I hit you," the fat Russian said. He laughed. "This is the famous killer? I'm not impressed."

Armin gave him a look. "The drug dealer is dead. The man we sent for her? The police found his body. Do not be *glupyy*, Dimitri." I knew that word: it's Russian for "stupid."

Armin yanked me to my feet. "Someone might be awake in one of those apartments," he said, nodding his head toward the buildings along the boardwalk. "Take her over to the benches. He should be here in a few minutes."

We headed down the boardwalk to a covered sitting area, passing a bent metal beach chair with torn green-and-white striped cloth. Fat Dimitri kept poking his Glock into my back. He was too close, and I was pretty sure I could take it from him. But Armin probably had a gun as well as a knife and would shoot me before I could get Dimitri's gun.

Dimitri shoved me down on a bench under the metal awning. He sat down facing me and wiped his face. He glanced at Armin. "Where is he?"

Armin shrugged. "Give me your phone."

"I left it in our car," Dimitri answered.

Armin made a *fuff* noise. "Why did you leave it there? That was stupid."

"And where is your phone, Armin?"

Armin made a *fuff* noise again then headed back to the boardwalk. A black Mercedes was parked behind Grandpa's Buick.

I bent over double, groaning. "I don't feel good. I think I'm sick."

"It will pass," Dimitri said. He sat down heavily on the bench across from me, pointing the Glock in my general direction. Over his shoulder, I saw the inside light in the Mercedes go off and Armin stepping off the boardwalk and walking back to us across the sand. I had maybe five seconds.

I knew that someone wanted me dead. *But I am Deborah Sokolov. I am not dying today.*